MEET THE FORTUNES!

Fortune of the Month: Toby Fortune Jones

Age: 28

Vital Statistics: Dazzling blue eyes, broad, strapping shoulders, strong arms that could hold a woman all night long...

Claim to Fame: Has a heart bigger than Texas.

Romantic Prospects: He's raising three foster kids *and* running a ranch. Are you kidding?

"I must be the king of bad timing. I finally meet a gal that's something special, and my nights are tied up with math homework and braiding pigtails. Angie is the first woman who seems to 'get' me. But let's be real. How many females are really in the market for a family of five? Forget about settling down—I haven't even been able to *kiss* her proper. How's a guy supposed to get to first base when there's always a first-grader underfoot?"

* * *

**THE FORTUNES OF TEXAS:
Welcome to Horseback Hollow!**

Dear Reader,

Welcome to Horseback Hollow! This is the fifth Fortunes of Texas series I've had the pleasure of working on, and while each series has been a lot of fun, I have to admit, writing *A House Full of Fortunes!* has been my most favorite of all.

Some people might think that I enjoyed this book and found it so easy to write because I have five children of my own—several of whom are redheads and prone to mischief. They might also tell you that I've known a few competitive gamblers in the day—characters a bit like Mr. Murdock.

All of that may be true, but there's just something about those Fortunes and Mendozas that always brings a smile to my face. And whether the stories are based in Red Rock or, in this case, Horseback Hollow, authors and readers alike know when they pick up a Fortunes of Texas book, they're in for a heartwarming romance and another amazing read.

So sit back, pour yourself a glass of sweetened iced tea and enjoy a few chuckles and some heartwarming smiles as Toby Fortune Jones tries his best to create a loving home for the three Hemings kids. And with the help of Angie Edwards, he'll find romance in the process.

Happy reading!

Judy

A House Full of Fortunes!

Judy Duarte

HARLEQUIN®SPECIAL EDITION®

Special thanks to Judy Duarte for her contribution to The Fortunes of Texas: Welcome to Horseback Hollow! continuity.

Recycling programs
for this product may
not exist in your area.

ISBN-13: 978-0-373-65805-3

A HOUSE FULL OF FORTUNES!

Printed in U.S.A.

JUDY DUARTE

always knew there was a book inside her, but since English was her least favorite subject in school, she never considered herself a writer. An avid reader who enjoys a happy ending, Judy couldn't shake the dream of creating a book of her own.

Her dream became a reality in March 2002, when Silhouette Special Edition released her first book, *Cowboy Courage*. Since then she has published more than twenty novels. Her stories have touched the hearts of readers around the world. And in July 2005 Judy won a prestigious Readers' Choice Award for *The Rich Man's Son*.

Judy makes her home near the beach in Southern California. When she's not cooped up in her writing cave, she's spending time with her somewhat enormous but delightfully close family.

To my daughter, Christy Duarte,
who has been an awesome critique partner,
brainstorm wizard and editor. You are a creative
and talented author who will soon hold your first
of many of your published books in your hands.
I love you, T.

Chapter One

"Justin! Get down from there!"

At the sound of the baritone voice spiked with irritation, Angie Edwards looked up from the cash register, stopped totaling her mother's grocery purchases and looked across the Superette to see a little red-haired boy high atop the stock clerk's ladder.

She was just about to rush over to the child before he fell when she spotted Toby Fortune Jones standing near the bottom rung, waiting for the little imp to climb down.

Toby, who owned a small ranch just outside of town and volunteered his time as a coach at the YMCA in nearby Vicker's Corners, had become a foster parent to the three Hemings children last fall.

Who would have guessed that the hunky rancher had such a paternal side? Just seeing him with those kids each time they came into the Superette gave Angie pause. And it warmed her heart, too.

What didn't warm her heart, however, was her mother checking up on her. Again.

"Don't forget that you're always welcome to come stay at my house if you need to," Angie's mother said, drawing her back to the task and the conversation at hand.

Angie loved her mom—she truly did—but there was no way she'd ever consider living with the woman again. There were times she couldn't get her mom off the telephone or, in this case, through the Superette checkout line fast enough for comfort.

"That'll be fourteen dollars and seventeen cents," Angie said, after she'd finished totaling her mother's purchases.

Why would Doris Edwards, who now lived and worked in Lubbock as a real-estate agent, drive all the way into Horseback Hollow to buy fifteen dollars' worth of groceries?

To check up on Angie and give her another lecture, no doubt. Thank goodness no one had gotten into line behind her yet.

"You're twenty-four and you can't work at the Superette forever." Her mother reached into her purse for her wallet. "Not that you've worked anywhere longer than a few months, but how are you ever going to make ends meet if you're only putting in four hours a day? Your rent will be due soon. I hope you have enough money set aside to cover it."

She did, but just barely. However, she'd learned early in life that it was best not to share her worries or concerns with her mom. The woman stressed about things entirely too much as it was. And nothing Angie did would ever be good enough for a hardworking powerhouse like Doris Edwards.

"I'll be fine. Really." Angie glanced around the grocery store, hoping the owners—Julia Tierney or her parents, Mr. and Mrs. Tierney—weren't within earshot. When she saw that they weren't, she slowly released a sigh of relief. "I knew this was a part-time position when I accepted it."

"You put in your application at The Hollows Cantina like I told you to, right?" As Doris pulled out a twenty-dollar bill, Angie nodded her confirmation that she had reluctantly applied.

"Well, at least that's something promising. From what I've heard, it's going to be an upscale place to eat."

If truth be told, Angie really had no interest in waiting tables. She'd already done that gig and, as much as Angie liked to cook, the restaurant business wasn't for her. Unfortunately, working part-time at the Superette and filling in as a receptionist at the flight school and charter service barely enabled her to make ends meet. Thank goodness she'd moved recently and had worked out a deal with her new landlord.

"You realize," Doris added, "that with the Fortune name behind the cantina, and with Jeanne Marie Fortune Jones being related to royalty and all… Well, you know what that means. People with money will be eating there. So it'll be a good place for you to network and make some connections. Then again, if it's a husband you want, your prospects will be better there than here. After all, if you want to catch a big fish, you have to go where they're swimming."

Angie blew out a sigh. Her mother had been pushing her to get the college degree she'd never gotten for herself. And since Angie usually found jobs through friends or through a temp agency in Vicker's Corners, her mother had decided she lacked the ambition to succeed in life. So Doris had recently started pushing a white-lace and gold-band solution.

But Angie wasn't looking for love. Not until she had a good idea of who she really was and where she was going in life.

She just wished her mother's voice wasn't so loud, and that she wouldn't make those kinds of comments in public.

"Why don't you come over for supper tonight," her mother said, as she reached for her grocery bag. "If you do, I'll fix meat loaf."

Angie would rather have a root canal than spend the evening with her mom, especially if she was making meat loaf. The woman had never been known for her domestic skills. Or her parenting skills, for that matter. In fact, Angie had probably cooked more of the family meals growing up than she had.

But it wasn't the quality of the food that would keep her away. It was the heartburn and the headache she expected to get from the mealtime conversation. As usual, her mom was sure to point out that Angie's only hope—at least, as far as Doris could see—was for Angie to snag a gainfully employed husband. And there was no reason to believe tonight would be any different. They'd had this conversation at least twenty times in the past couple of months.

To be honest, Angie feared that at least some of what her mother believed might be true. Not that she needed a man to rescue her. That certainly wasn't the case. But for some reason, Angie just couldn't seem to get fired up about anything, which she found troubling. Because at twenty-four, you'd think she'd know what she wanted to do with her life.

Angie had never been good with decisions of any kind, as was evident by her résumé, which read like a copy of the Yellow Pages. But why pour herself into something when her heart wasn't in it? She always figured she'd know what she was meant to do with her life when she felt some sort of spark or passion. Until then, she'd just keep trying a little bit of everything and commit to nothing.

The sound of broken glass sounded from the first aisle, followed by a little girl's shriek.

"I'm sorry!" This came from a boy—maybe the one who'd been on the ladder. "But it wasn't my fault, Toby. Kylie pushed me into the stack of mayonnaise. I didn't mean to knock the jars over."

Angie reached for the small microphone to the right of her register. "Ralph? We'll need a cleanup at the front of aisle one."

Poor Toby. His foster kids were usually pretty well-mannered, but they were obviously having a bad day. At least, the middle boy was.

"Thank goodness you don't have *that* problem to worry about, Evangeline." Her mother shot a look of annoyance at the mayonnaise mess and then at the three children arguing over who was at fault. "Women like us were *not* meant to stay at home and raise a passel of rug rats. I can't imagine what Toby was thinking when he took in that brood."

The soft dark hairs on the back of Angie's neck bristled at her mother's familiar rant against children. *Just ignore it,* Angie thought. She knew better than to engage Doris in a conversation like that, especially in public.

"I'm sorry, Mom. I can't do dinner tonight. I already have plans." Angie just hoped her mother didn't ask what those plans might be because she'd probably spend the first half of her evening looking in her pantry trying to decide what to eat and the second half sitting in front of the television, wearing out the remote.

"Oh, really?" Doris perked up. "What are you doing tonight?"

So much for hoping her mother wouldn't ask.

As the next customer began to place his groceries on the conveyor belt, Angie tore her gaze from her mom and glanced at Toby, the man who'd gotten in line behind her. In spite of those gorgeous baby blues and the kind of face that made even strangers want to confide in him, Toby looked a bit frazzled today.

Funny. He usually looked so capable and put-together.

"I'll have to give you a call and we can talk more later," Angie told her mother. "We don't want to hold up the line."

"Sure, honey." Doris glanced over her shoulder. When she spotted Toby, she offered him a sympathetic smile. "You've certainly got your hands full."

"Just enough to keep life interesting—and fun."

Toby tossed Doris a boyish grin, then winked at Angie as if the two of them were in on a secret.

Being included, even in a make-believe secret, was enough to lift Angie's spirits and to trigger a smile of her own.

"We're going fishing," Brian, the older boy, said. "That is, if there're any fish left by the time we get to Cutter's Pond."

Toby placed a hand on the boy's shoulder. "Nonsense. Everyone knows the bigger fish are busy fattening themselves up and waiting for just the right person to come and catch them up." Toby winked at Angie again, and she realized he must have overheard her mother's comment about fishing for a suitable mate while working at The Hollows Cantina.

As her cheeks warmed, she looked at the small space under the cash register, wishing she could stuff her five-foot-seven-inch body into the square opening.

But why stress about it? It wasn't as though she'd set her sights on Toby as a viable romantic option. He was practically the guy next door.

She'd known the Jones family—make that the *Fortune* Jones family—forever. She'd gone to school with Toby's sister Stacey, although they'd never run in the same circles. She'd even double-dated with Toby's brother Jude a couple of times, but there'd never been any sparks, so nothing had ever come of it.

Toby was probably the only one of Stacey's hunky brothers Angie hadn't considered dating.

Not that he wasn't just as handsome as the others. Angie looked at his tall frame, lean and muscled from years of ranch work and extracurricular sports coaching. Yep, Toby Fortune Jones could definitely compete with his brothers in the looks department.

But Toby always seemed so confident and so sure of himself. And people who knew exactly what they wanted and went after it always intimidated her. Plus, the whole "Mother Teresa meets Dudley Do-Right" personality only made Toby seem all the more out of reach.

A guy like Toby would never be interested in someone like her. He'd want a woman who was down-to-earth, a woman who had her ducks in a row.

Someone who had dreams and plans to fulfill. Someone who wouldn't ever stress about what job she was going to try next.

Angie's mother reached for her grocery bag, causing Angie to break her bold perusal.

"Must be nice to have so much free time on your hands," Doris said to Toby. "Have fun."

Angie could see the disapproval evident on her mom's face. Doris Edwards didn't believe in burning daylight simply for fishing or spending time with one's family.

"We will," Toby told her. "You have a nice day, Mrs. Edwards."

As Doris headed to the parking lot, she turned back to look at what Angie was wearing behind the check stand. "And, honey," Doris said reproachingly, her voice quieter yet still loud enough for anyone within five feet of her to hear, "try to dress a bit more conservatively. Nobody is going to take you seriously with all those curves popping out everywhere. You look like you just got off a shift at a roadhouse honky-tonk."

Doris's smartphone rang, thankfully cutting off her insult to Angie's snug-but-comfortable jeans and her white T-shirt. "Gotta take this. You know, the client always comes first."

Angie started the conveyor belt as her mother breezed out the door in a conservative shoulder-padded power suit. She tried to smile through the mortification that warmed her cheeks and strained the muscles in her face. "Chips, soda, cookies... Looks like someone is planning a picnic."

Toby tossed her a playful grin. "Fishing on the lake is hungry business."

"It should be a nice day for it," Angie said, as she began to check out Toby—or rather, his groceries.

Not that there wasn't plenty to check out about the man himself—if she were looking.

Brown hair that was stylishly mussed, but not out of place. Dazzling blue eyes that were both playful and bright. Broad, strapping shoulders. Arms that looked as though they could pitch a mean curveball—or hold a woman tightly all night.

"I don't want to go to Cutter's Pond," Kylie complained, breaking Angie from her wayward thoughts. "You're just going to kill those poor fish. And I don't even like to eat them."

Brian rolled his eyes. "Don't be such a stinking crybaby, Kylie. We never get to do anything fun without you complaining."

Toby glanced at Angie and gave a little shrug. "Sometimes it's hard to find an activity or an outing they can all enjoy. It seems that someone always has an objection."

Angie smiled. "To be honest, I can't blame her a bit. I never did like putting a worm on a hook."

"You had to go fishing, too?" the little red-haired girl asked.

Angie offered her a sympathetic smile. "When my father was alive, he would take me to Cutter's Pond. And while I could usually count on getting sunburned and bit by a mosquito or two, there was always something special about spending time with my daddy."

"But I don't have a daddy," the girl said.

Angie's cheeks warmed. She'd only wanted to help, but had probably made things worse.

"You might not have a dad," Toby said, as he gave one of Kylie's lopsided auburn pigtails a gentle tug, "but you have *me*."

Toby's hands might be skilled at lassoing horses and throwing a football, but the poor man couldn't do a little girl's hair to save his life.

Still, these kids were lucky to have Toby. If he hadn't stepped up to the plate when their aunt had gone off the deep end and lost custody, they might have been separated and placed in different foster homes.

Justin, the boy who'd climbed the ladder, said, "Too bad we don't have a babysitter for Kylie. She's gonna wah-wah like a little crybaby and ruin our whole day." Justin made fake crying noises and rubbed his eyes to emphasize his overly dramatic point.

Maybe Angie could help out after all. "I only have to work for a half hour or so, and then my shift is over. If you don't mind leaving Kylie here with me, I'd be happy to hang out with her while you and the boys go fishing. We can do cool girls-only things that boys don't get to do."

"That's nice of you to offer," Toby said, "but you don't have to do that."

"Yes, she does!" Kylie gave a little jump and a clap.

Uh-oh. What had Angie done? Had she overstepped her boundaries—or bitten off more than she could chew?

"*Please,* Toby?" Kylie looked at her foster dad with puppy-dog eyes. "Can I stay here with Angie? Can I *please?*"

"If you're sure you don't mind." Toby's gaze zeroed in on Angie, and her heart spun in her chest.

What was that little zing all about?

Had that come from the way Toby was looking at her? Or from having second thoughts about what she'd just offered to do?

After all, she didn't know anything about kids. She'd been an only child and Doris definitely wasn't the maternal type. Plus, unlike some of the other girls she'd grown up with, she'd never even had a babysitting job.

But now that she'd made the offer, she couldn't very well backpedal.

"Of course I don't mind." Angie reached under the checkout stand for a stack of coloring pages and pulled out the top sheet. "The Superette is having a poster contest this month. All the kids have to do is color this picture and turn it back in for the judging. I have a few markers Kylie can use. Then, after I clock out, we'll be on our way for the best girls' day ever!"

Toby shot her an appreciative smile. "All right. We'll

probably only be a couple of hours. Where should I pick her up?"

Angie hadn't given much thought to what she'd do with Kylie, but since she didn't have any money to spend, they'd have to find something cheap to do at home. "I live in the small granny flat behind Elmer Murdock's place. Do you know where that is?"

"Sure do. Mr. Murdock owns the yellow, two-story house next to the post office. I didn't know anyone was living in that…unit in the back."

It wasn't common knowledge. In fact, she hadn't even mentioned the move to her mother yet.

Should she explain her living situation? Or better yet, make an excuse for it?

She decided to do neither.

After totaling Toby's purchases, Angie took his cash and gave him his change. Then she watched him leave the store with the boys, walking with that same swagger the other Fortune Jones boys possessed.

No, she'd never considered dating Toby in the past. And for the briefest of moments, she wondered why she hadn't.

After a fun but unproductive day at Cutter's Pond, Toby and the boys climbed into his truck. If they wanted fish for supper tonight, Toby would have to make another stop at the Superette and purchase a few fillets. As it was, he decided to make things easy on himself and to take the kids to The Horseback Hollow Grill for a couple of burgers. But first they'd have to pick up Kylie.

It had been nice of Angie to offer to babysit. The

afternoon had been a lot more pleasant with only the boys. Not that Kylie was a problem child. She was a sweetheart most of the time, but… Well, she had a tendency to get a little teary when things didn't go her way. But he supposed he couldn't really blame her. It had to be tough for a little girl growing up in a boys' world.

As he pulled his black four-wheel-drive Dodge Ram along the curb in front of the old Murdock place, he scanned the front yard, which looked a lot better than it had the last time he'd driven by. The once-overgrown lawn had been mowed recently and a sprinkler had brought the grass back to life.

The old house was still in need of repair—or at least, a fresh coat of paint and some new shutters. But that wasn't surprising. Elmer Murdock was well over eighty years old and living on his marine-corps retirement pay.

"Can we get out, too?" Justin asked.

"I don't see why not." While they'd all had a blast fishing, Toby knew the boys had been stewing over what kind of things might constitute a "girls-only" day. Apparently, the mystery of womanhood began early in a male's life.

He shut off the ignition, got out of the pickup and made his way to the path that led to the back of the house, where Mr. Murdock had built separate quarters for his widowed mother-in-law decades ago.

The "granny flat," as Angie had called it, was even more run-down than the main house. The small porch railing had come loose and was about to collapse, although the wood flooring had been swept recently.

A pot of red geraniums added a splash of color to the chipped and weathered white paint.

Brian and Justin lagged behind by several feet because they'd stopped to check out two different birdhouses in a maple tree. The birdhouse on the left was pretty basic, but the one on the right was three stories with a wraparound porch and looked like something straight out of his mother's *Southern Living* magazine.

Toby continued to the front door and knocked loud enough to be heard over the sound of Taylor Swift belting out her latest hit. He cringed, although he knew that, as a proud Texan, he should favor country music, even crossover pop artists like Taylor Swift. But his well-guarded secret was that he couldn't stand the stuff. He preferred his music with a lot more soul and a lot less twang.

When the front door swung open, Kylie, her face smeared with green goo, greeted Toby with a bright-eyed smile. "Guess what? Mr. Murdock and Angie had a nail-painting contest and I got to be the judge. And see, Mr. Murdock won because he painted the cutest little horse on my big toenail." She lifted her right leg high in the air in an effort to put her toe in front of his face.

"Yeah, well, Mr. Murdock cheated," came Angie's reply. "He took an hour to do it, using a magnifying glass and his model-airplane paint, which, by the way, isn't washable. That horse will never come off."

Toby couldn't actually see Angie, since she had her back to the door and was leaning over the arm of the sofa, a white container in one hand and a green sponge in the other.

Both amused and touched by the sight, Toby couldn't help but chuckle.

"Ooh, gross," Brian said, when he spotted his sister's face. "What happened to you?"

"I'm getting pretty—just like Angie."

Both boys began to hoot and howl.

Toby couldn't say that he blamed them. Kylie, who was a cutie-pie when she wasn't whining, looked like a pint-sized version of the creature from the black lagoon, walking around with a green face and her fingers and toes splayed out wide so the paint would dry.

The little red-haired girl stepped aside to allow them into the small house, just as Angie straightened. As Toby's eyes landed on Angie's face, it appeared as though she'd climbed from the same lagoon.

She smiled as if having green goop smeared all over wasn't the least bit unusual. "We didn't expect you back so soon."

"It certainly appears that way." Toby couldn't help but laugh.

"Just for the record, I did not cheat. You never established any ground rules." Elmer Murdock sprang up from the sofa Angie had been leaning over, the same green mud on his face. And Toby didn't know whether he should hoot with laughter or try his best to hold it back.

Was this the formidable retired marine who'd instilled fear in most of Horseback Hollow High School's youth with his loud shouting during football practices?

And for some reason, the old leatherneck didn't seem to be the least bit embarrassed at being caught having a facial.

Mr. Murdock slapped his hands on his hips and ze-roed in on Angie. "I didn't complain about *you* cheat-ing when you used way more material on that Bird McMansion than I did during our birdhouse-building contest."

Toby quickly grabbed his ball cap from his head and pulled it lower over his face to cover his smirk. Was this the one-and-only Elmer Murdock?

His brothers would never believe this.

"You built that huge birdhouse outside?" Brian asked Angie. "I didn't know girls could build like that."

"Girls can do anything. Especially *this* girl." Angie pointed to her green-covered face. "I got an A in wood-shop when I was in high school. Give me a hammer, wood and nails, and I can build anything."

"Can you help me build my car for the soapbox derby?" Brian asked.

"Only if you want to win," Angie replied. Then she pointed to the sofa. "Have a seat, guys. Mr. Murdock has a few more minutes for his face to dry, but it's time for us ladies to wash off our masks. We'll be back in a Flash, Gordon."

"Hey," Brian said. "*Flash Gordon.* That's funny."

Toby crossed his arms and shifted his weight to one hip. Wow, Brian had been pretty quiet and distant ever since the state had stepped in and removed the kids from their aunt's custody. But he'd warmed up to Angie in about three minutes flat.

As Angie led Kylie across the small living area that served as both kitchen and sitting room, Toby couldn't help but watch the brunette who wore a pair of cutoff jeans that would have put Daisy Duke to shame pad across the floor. Her hips moved in a natural sway, her long, shapely legs damn near perfect. He remembered Doris Edwards's cutting potshot at the Superette and thought that from where he was standing, there was absolutely nothing wrong with Angie's curves.

He continued to watch her from behind until she and Kylie disappeared into the only other room in the house and shut the door.

Justin was sitting next to Mr. Murdock and reaching out his fingers to the wrinkled weather-beaten cheek. "Is that mud?" he asked the old man.

"Justin," Toby scolded, "keep your hands to yourself."

"Yeah, but this is sissy mud," Mr. Murdock answered casually. "It's supposed to clear your pores and detoxify your skin or some such bull. I'll tell you what, we never worried about our pores when we were covered in mud back in that wet foxhole in Korea. All we cared about was not getting our fool heads blown off."

"Wow, you got shot at in a war?" Brian asked as Justin started using the white container to apply stripes to his own eight-year-old face in a war-paint fashion that would make any Apache proud.

"Mr. Murdock," Angie yelled from the bathroom at the end of the small hall, "stop talking so much. You need to keep still and let the mask dry. Every time you talk, you crack it."

Mr. Murdock clamped his thin lips together in their perpetual grimace.

As Toby scanned Angie's small living area, he couldn't help but take note of the freshly painted blue walls that had been adorned with the oddest forms of artwork—

the label side of a wooden produce crate that advertised Parnell's Apple Farm, an old mirror framed with pieces of broken ceramic, a coatrack made out of doorknobs...

She'd placed a whitewashed bookshelf against one wall. Instead of books, it held various knickknacks. A bouquet of bluebonnets in a Mason jar sat on top. The furniture was old, and while the decor was kind of funky, the house had a cozy appeal.

"So you're running the old Double H Ranch?" Mr. Murdock asked Toby, lasting only a couple of minutes before he broke Angie's orders to stay quiet. It was hard to take the crotchety old man seriously with the green mud caked onto his face and his lips barely able to move.

"Sure am," Toby replied, warming up to his favorite subject—his ranch. "We have more than three hundred head of cattle now, and I've been doing some breeding."

"I used to do some roping back before I enlisted, you know. Could probably still out-rope most of you young upstarts. I should swing by your place and we could have a little contest."

What was it with this old man and contests? Apparently his competitiveness went well beyond the high-school football field.

Before Toby could politely decline the challenge, the door swung open and the girls came out.

Angie had apparently swapped the denim shorts for a yellow floral sundress, yet she was still barefoot, her toenails painted the same pink shade as Kylie's— minus the horse.

"We had a really good day," Angie said, her face clean, her eyes bright.

"We did, too," he said.

"Did you catch anything?"

"I'm afraid not."

"I used to catch all kinds of stuff out at Cutter's Pond," Mr. Murdock chimed in, while the boys continued to stare at the old swamp monster look-alike as if he were a real hero come to life. "Still hold the record for the biggest trout ever caught in Horseback Hollow. Nobody's beat me yet."

"Okay, Mr. Murdock, you should be dry." Angie patted her landlord on his shoulder. "You can probably go home and wash your face now."

"Roger that," the old coot replied as he shuffled toward the door and back to the main house. The former marine looked like a strong Texas wind would knock him over, and Toby doubted the man was in any shape to rope a tractor on his ranch, let alone a longhorn steer, although he'd never say so out loud.

Instead, he nodded at the interior of Angie's little house, at the freshly painted blue walls. "I like what you've done with this place. You certainly have a creative side."

"You think so? Thanks." She scanned the cramped quarters, too. "The house was empty for nearly twenty years, so it was pretty stuffy and drab when I moved in. I spent a couple of days cleaning and airing it out. I've also learned how to decorate on a shoestring budget, which has been fun."

"I can see that. You've done a great job. Where did you find this stuff?"

"Some of it was already here—like the furniture. I picked up the paint on sale when I was in Vicker's Corners the other day. Someone had ordered the wrong color, so it was practically free. I've also been picking up odds and ends at garage sales. Then I figured out a way to make them pretty—or at least, interesting."

"I'm impressed. You're quite the homemaker."

She brightened, and her wholesome beauty stunned him. Not that he hadn't noticed before, but he'd never seen her blue eyes light up when she smiled like that.

"To tell you the truth," he added, "I was surprised to hear that you'd moved in here. The windows had been boarded up for ages, and the weeds had grown up so high that most people forgot that there was a little house back here at all."

"Mr. Murdock and I were talking one day at the Superette, and he mentioned that he needed to hire someone to do some chores for him. I told him I had some free time. And when I spotted the little house, I asked if he'd be interested in renting it to me."

"I'd think you would have preferred to find a place that wouldn't have required as much work."

She shrugged. "Let's just say that, like Mr. Murdock, I love a challenge. Besides, his sons live out of state, so he's all alone. Plus, this way, I can look out for him and let him think he's looking out for me."

Toby had always thought Angie was a bit shallow, although he couldn't say why he'd come to that conclusion. Probably because he'd heard a few people say that she was flighty. But apparently, he'd been wrong. There was more to her than he'd given her credit for.

He also owed her for taking care of Kylie today, although something told him she wouldn't accept any money for doing it. So it seemed like the most natural thing in the world to say, "We're going to have burgers at The Grill. Would you like to join us?"

And it seemed even more natural for her to respond, "Sure. Why not?"

Chapter Two

The Horseback Hollow Grill, which was attached to the Two Moon Saloon, wasn't much to shout about when it came to eateries. But it was one of the only options in town. Fortunately, they served the juiciest burgers and dogs, fresh-cut fries and a mean grilled-cheese sandwich.

As Angie climbed from Toby's lifted truck, she couldn't help but smile. If her mom could see her now, the poor woman would be torn between deep anxiety and despair.

First of all, she'd be dancing on clouds to see Angie enter a restaurant with one of the Fortune Jones men, even if it was only The Grill. Doris assumed all the Fortunes were wealthy beyond their wildest dreams, although local rumor had it that the Horseback Hollow branch of the family hadn't struck any gold.

According to what Angie had heard, Jeanne Marie Fortune Jones had been adopted. And when her birth brother, James Marshall Fortune, had found her last year, he'd given her a portion of his stock in the family company. But when she found out those shares were supposed to go to his kids, she'd refused it.

Nevertheless, even with a boatload of cash, a man with three kids wasn't the catch Angie's mom had been hoping she'd snag.

Of course, this wasn't a date by any stretch of the word. Toby had only included her in the family plans because he was a nice guy. And Angie had accepted because she'd had nothing better to do and was on an especially tight budget these days.

As they entered the small-town restaurant, where artificial flowers in hammered coffeepots sat on old-style tables with rounded edges encased in silver metal, Angie realized they weren't the only ones in Horseback Hollow who'd decided to pick up a quick meal tonight. The place was certainly hopping.

Toby nodded toward an empty booth by the window, one of the few places to sit that weren't taken.

"Can we play in the game room for a while?" Justin asked.

Angie remembered the small arcade in back—if you could call it that—from her own school days. Back then, The Grill was *the* place to hang out if you were a teenager in Horseback Hollow. It probably still was, so she couldn't blame the kids for their eagerness to drop coins into the video-game machines.

"What do you guys want to eat?" he asked.

"I'd like grilled cheese," Kylie said, "but only if they have real bread and square cheese."

Angie cocked her head slightly. "What's she talking about?"

Toby chuckled. "We stopped at a place in Lubbock one day, and they brought out a sandwich that had been made with focaccia bread and several fancy kinds of cheese. It was the restaurant's claim to fame, and it cost a pretty penny, but Kylie didn't like it. By 'square' cheese, she means good ole American slices, individually wrapped."

"Aw." Angie smiled. "I'll have to remember that."

"I want a corn dog and fries," Justin said.

"Got it." Toby turned to Brian. "How about you?"

"I want a cheeseburger, but I don't want onions or lettuce or pickles. But ask if they'll give me extra tomatoes."

"Since we've got that out of the way, here you go." Toby reached into his pocket and pulled out a small handful of quarters. "Why don't you start with these? I'll get some change after the waitress takes our order."

While the kids dashed off, Toby waited for Angie to slide into the booth, then did the same.

As she settled into a middle spot, he removed his ball cap, as any proper Texan gentleman would do, leaving his brown hair disarrayed and close to his head. She was tempted to reach out and finger-comb it.

Or maybe she just wanted to touch it and see if it was as soft as it looked.

Odd, though. He didn't appear to be the least bit… mussed. He actually looked darn near perfect.

As if completely unaware of her perusal—and why

wouldn't he be?—he reached across the table for the menus and handed her one, ending her silly musing.

But as she opened it up and scanned the offerings—burgers, hot dogs and sandwiches—her options, while too few by some people's standards, still seemed too difficult to narrow down.

This was the part about eating out that she dreaded. She could never decide on what to order, especially when there were other people with her.

Since she didn't want Toby to think that she was indecisive, she did what she'd learned to do on her other dates. Not that this was a date.

Or was it? Did *Toby* think it was a date?

The waitress, a tall brunette in her early forties, approached. "What'll it be?"

Toby placed the kids' orders, then asked Angie, "What would you like?"

She gave her standard reply. "I'll have whatever you're having."

But when Toby ordered the double bacon cheeseburger, the large onion rings, fried pickles and jumbo peanut-butter milk shake, she realized she'd have to rethink her strategy if she ever went to another restaurant with him again.

Where was she going to put all that food?

"Maybe you'd better not bring me those pickles," she told the waitress.

The woman nodded, then made a note on her pad. After she left them alone, things got a little quiet. Actually, too quiet, since Angie tended to get bored easily.

So she said, "Looks like the kids will be busy for a while."

He smiled. "I remember when those games were brand-new. Fifteen years later, and they're still entertaining kids."

"You might not believe this," Angie said, "but I was a whiz at Ms. Pac-Man. There weren't too many people who could outscore me."

"Not even Mr. Murdock?"

At that, Angie laughed and shook her head. "Please don't tell him. I've never met a man more competitive than he is. If he finds out, I'll be forced to defend my title."

"Wow! A *titleholder?*" Toby tossed her a heart-strumming grin. "Who would have guessed that I'd be sharing a meal with a real live champion?"

"Yeah, well, it'd be nice to have a more worthwhile claim to fame than 'Top Scorer on Ms. Pac-Man.'" Angie settled back in the booth. Even the praise over what little she had achieved in life didn't do much in the way of soothing her embarrassment over her mother's public criticism.

"I'm sure you have plenty of things to be proud of," he said.

Their gazes met and held for a moment. Her smile faded, and she broke eye contact.

She was also a champ at changing subjects.

"The kids certainly seem to be settling in," she said.

"They seem to be. It was tough for a while, though. Justin was acting out and getting in trouble at school, but he's doing better now. And Kylie no longer has nightmares. Brian still holds back a bit, although I can understand that. It's hard for him to trust adults. Each one he's ever had to depend on has abandoned him—one way or another."

She'd heard a few scant rumors about the kids, but she didn't know what was true and what wasn't.

"What happened to their mother?" she asked.

"She was diagnosed with cancer right after Kylie was born and died just before her first birthday. Justin was only two at the time, so Brian's the only one who was old enough to remember her."

"What about their dad?"

Toby glanced toward the arcade, where the kids continued to play. Still, he kept his voice low. "From what I understand, he wasn't the kind of guy who could handle responsibility. When Ann, their mom, found out that she was pregnant with Kylie, he left her. And no one has heard from him since."

"That's so sad." Angie had always been close to her father, and when her parents had split up, it had crushed her. Losing her dad to cancer two years later had been even worse.

"After Ann died," Toby continued, "the kids went to live with her sister. But Barbara wasn't prepared for the challenge of raising two toddlers and a five-year-old. She drank as a way of escape. And the kids seemed to exacerbate her stress—and her need for the bottle."

"When did the state step in?" Angie asked.

"Last year, when Justin's behavioral problems in school escalated. The authorities were called in to investigate, and that's when they found out how bad things were at home. Shortly after that, Barbara was arrested. At that point, she was ordered to get in-patient treatment and the children were placed in separate fos-

ter homes. I hated the thought of them being split up.
Family is important. And they'd lost so much already.
So I volunteered to take them in."

"That was a big step for a bachelor."

He shrugged. "My mom was adopted. It just seemed
like a natural way to pay it forward."

There it was again. Toby's altruistic personality. Everything about him was too perfect. Even his slightly
mussed hair, which she was still tempted to reach out
and touch.

It had a bit of a curl to it. Was it *really* as soft as it
looked?

Oh, good grief. Get a grip, girl. She forced herself
to stop gawking at him and to keep the conversation
going. "So how long have you had them? About six
months?"

"Yes, and I'll be the first to admit that it was a big
adjustment. But it's getting easier. I actually like having them around. The ranch was too quiet before. You
probably can imagine what it was like for me, growing
up with all my brothers and sisters. I'm used to noise.
Sometimes I feel as if I can't concentrate unless the
decibel level is over ninety-five."

Actually, Angie couldn't imagine what any of that
had been like. She didn't have any siblings. So her
house had always been as quiet as a tomb, unless she
had friends over.

"It was the talk of the town when you got custody
of the kids," she said. "Most people didn't think it
would last."

"My buddies certainly didn't think it would."

"How about you?" she asked. "How are you holding up?"

"I'm doing all right, but it's put a real cramp in my social life."

Angie smiled. "You mean with the guys—or romantically speaking?"

"Romance? What's that?" Toby laughed. "Actually, if I were even in a position to be looking for a relationship, I'd be in a real fix. Most women go running for the hills when they hear I have three children, even though the situation is supposed to be temporary. Other women look at me as if I'm some kind of hero. But even then, when they're faced with the reality of dating a man with the responsibility of three kids, they don't stick around long."

Point taken. Toby was making it clear that he wasn't looking for a relationship. Therefore, Angie now knew this clearly wasn't a date.

"Yet here you are," she said, "out with the kids having burgers, when you could be having a few beers at the Two Moon Saloon and dancing with Horseback Hollow's most eligible bachelorettes. From what I remember, you were always a pretty good dancer."

"I still am. Maybe I'll prove it to you sometime." Now, that was a challenge Angie looked forward to. And while the boyish grin on his face suggested that he was teasing, for a moment, for a heartbeat, she'd suspected that he'd been a wee bit serious.

And if they were ever to lay their secrets out on the table, she'd have to admit that she wouldn't mind dancing with him, holding him close, swaying to the slow beat of a country love song, her body pressed to his…

"Seriously, though," he said, drawing her back to reality, "if I wanted a beer, they'd serve me one in here. But I have enough on my plate without having to worry about dancing and courting the ladies, too."

"I hear you." And she did—loud and clear. He'd said it twice now, which was just as well. *Really,* it was. "I'm not looking for love, either—although my mother seems to think I should be."

"Doris is really hard on you. Why is that?"

"Because she's lost all hope of me making a financial success of my life. So if I can't be the money-making ballbuster she envisions, the least I can do is marry one."

"Well, then, Doris can rest assured that you'll be safe from me. I'm definitely not raking in the dough."

Safe from him? Toby couldn't be more obvious if he was wearing a blinking neon sign. She wanted to say, *Okay, I get it. You're not interested in me.*

But she supposed it wasn't necessary. Neither one of them was in any position to enter into a romantic relationship right now—with anyone.

"I wouldn't let your mother drag you down," Toby said. "You seem like a happy person. So whatever you're doing must be working for you."

Well, not exactly. While she wasn't miserable, she'd be a lot happier if she had a full-time job—or at least some direction.

"I'm doing just fine," she said.

Before Toby could respond, Kylie ran up to the table. "Brian won't let me have a turn driving the race car. He said it's 'cause I'm a girl. And 'cause my feet won't reach the pedals. But they will if he lets me sit on his lap."

"I have an idea," Angie said, as she slid out from behind the booth. "I'm going to show you how to play a better game. One that you can play all by yourself."

"You're coming in pretty handy," Toby said.

Angie laughed. "I'm just paying for my supper."

"At this rate, I'm going to owe you breakfast, too."

For a moment, just like the comment about dancing together had done, the overnight innuendo hung in the air. And while they both might have laughed it off, there'd been a brief moment when their gazes had met, a beat when she suspected that neither of them had taken the promise of an early-morning breakfast lightly.

Toby hoped the waitress brought their food soon. Not only was he hungry, but he was down to his last few quarters and wasn't about to ask for any more change than he had already. Since taking in the kids six months ago, his coin contributions alone could go a long way in refurbishing some of those old games and buying a new one.

He took a sip of his milk shake and watched the kids and Angie return to the table—out of quarters again, no doubt.

"You're pretty good at Ms. Pac-Man," Brian told Angie, as she slipped back into the booth.

"Thanks." She winked at Toby. "I used to be a lot better, but I'm getting rusty in my old age."

"You aren't that old," Justin said, taking her far more seriously than she'd intended. "Maybe if you came here to practice more often, you'd be supergood again."

Angie laughed. "I'm afraid my days of playing in the arcade are over."

"That's too bad," Justin said. "I'll bet you could hold the world record."

"I'll have to remind my mother that I actually have some talent the next time she worries about my future prospects."

"Here you go," Toby said, as he rationed out a few more of the coveted coins to the kids.

Then they dashed off, leaving him and Angie alone again. It was nice getting to know her, getting a chance to see a side to her he'd never realized was there. He didn't think he was the only one in town to have misconceptions about Angie Edwards. Heck, even her own mother didn't seem to appreciate her.

Toby hadn't liked the way her mom had talked to her today, especially in front of other people. But he supposed that wasn't any of his business. He'd always had a sympathetic nature. In fact, his brothers often ribbed him, saying he was a sucker for people who were down on their luck. Some of that might be true, although he didn't see Angie that way.

Sure, maybe she wasn't a superambitious go-getter. But she seemed to have a good head—and a pretty one at that—on her shoulders. And something told him that she'd find her groove in life soon.

"You know," he said, "it's not too late to go back to school."

"No, it isn't. But you're looking at a woman who'd joined the Toastmasters Club, the Teachers of Tomorrow, Health Careers and Future Farmers of America when I was in high school. I was even a member of the French Club one semester. I couldn't decide on a direction then, and I'm no closer to having one now. So I can't imagine spending the time and money to take classes without a goal in mind. So far, my motto in life has been 'just keep on keeping on.'"

"Well, if it makes you feel any better, I think that motto suits you pretty well. You're a lot of fun to be with. And you have a great ability to adapt. I'm sure you'll figure something out."

"Yes, but as each week passes, my mother gets more and more stressed about my future."

"How about you?" he asked. "Are you worried about it?"

She tossed him a pretty smile. "I'm doing just fine."

He didn't doubt that she was. "Then that ought to settle it."

She took her glass, wrapped her full lips around the straw and took a slow drag of her milk shake, making him think about somewhere else her mouth could be…

What in blazes was wrong with him? Angie Edwards wasn't the woman for him. He needed someone who was solid and stable, someone who was willing to take on three kids. And while Angie could probably handle anything life threw at her, she didn't seem like the type who would stick around for the long haul.

And even though everyone in town, including his family, thought that his taking on the Hemings kids was a temporary thing, Toby had gotten attached to them, and he wasn't planning to give them up unless their aunt insisted on taking them back. And even then, he wasn't sure if he'd step back without a fight. But from what he'd gathered from the social worker, their aunt Barbara wasn't the maternal type.

So if he had any chance of keeping them, he needed a partner who would be just as committed to the kids as he was.

Still, that didn't mean Angie wasn't an attractive woman. What she might lack in commitment, she more than made up for with sex appeal.

Yet the more time he spent with her, the more intriguing he found her.

Why hadn't he looked at her that way before? Well, of course he'd noticed her looks. He wasn't blind. But he'd never been the kind of guy to date someone just because of her physical appearance. He'd been interested in the woman on the inside.

Of course, after talking with her this evening, he had to admit that he was curious about what made her tick.

Even though they'd both grown up in Horseback Hollow, he really didn't know very much about her—except in the way that most folks in small towns knew stuff about each other.

Up until today, he and Angie had never said more than a few words to each other in passing.

Before he could ponder it any further, the waitress brought their food. While she was placing the plates on the table, Toby excused himself and went after the kids.

Moments later, they were all seated at the booth. The boys began to dig in, but Kylie merely looked at her plate and frowned.

"What's the matter?" Angie asked.

"It's too much. I don't want it."

"Oops," Toby said. "The boys are such good eaters that I sometimes forget about her. She isn't actually all that fussy, but I think she gets overwhelmed when her plate is too full."

"What if you share with me," Angie said. "Would that help?"

When Kylie nodded, Angie took a knife and, with a careful slice, cut the grilled cheese into quarters instead of halves. "I like smaller triangles. Don't you?"

The little girl smiled.

Angie reached for a section. "Can I have some of your fries, too?"

Again, Kylie nodded.

Toby would have to remember that trick.

Next, Angie took the knife, then sliced her double bacon burger in two. "When the waitress comes by I'm going to ask her for a to-go box."

"What are you going to do?" Toby asked. "Take that home for lunch tomorrow?"

"Actually, I thought I'd offer it to Mr. Murdock. He likes a late-night snack when he watches television. And I thought it would be a nice surprise."

So she was thoughtful, too—especially with kids and the elderly.

Toby took a bite of his burger, relishing the taste. No one made them better than The Grill.

"Can you hand me the mustard?" Angie asked.

Toby reached for the bottle that stood next to the menus on the table and handed it to her, thinking she was going to apply it to the portion of the burger she intended to eat. Instead, she poured a glob onto her plate, dipped one of the French fries into it and took a bite.

"Most people prefer catsup," he said. "Miss Edwards, you're proving to be quite a novelty."

She smiled. "'Always keep 'em guessing.' That's my motto."

Toby laughed. "You have a lot of mottos, I'm learning."

She tossed him a pretty smile.

"Can I try that?" Justin asked. "Pass me the mustard, too."

"I'm not going to be able to eat all these onion rings," Angie said. "Does anyone want to help me out?"

"I've never had them before," Brian said.

She passed her plate to him. "You should at least try one. You might be missing a real treat."

Ten minutes later, Kylie had eaten three-quarters of her sandwich. Justin had finished off his corn dog and decided that he preferred dipping his fries in mustard rather than catsup. And Brian had wolfed down most of Angie's onion rings.

Then the kids dashed back to the arcade with the last of the quarters, leaving the adults sitting amid the clutter of nearly empty plates, wadded napkins, dribbles of soda pop and a melting ice cube.

Toby studied Angie in the dim light of the least romantic restaurant in West Texas.

Why in the world hadn't he taken the time to get to know her sooner, when his life hadn't been complicated by three children?

He supposed one reason he'd steered clear of her

was because his brother Jude had once dated her. And for that reason, Toby had considered her off-limits.

Yet, when the kids returned to the table, high from their final top-ranking scores on Ms. Pac-Man, the sound of Angie's infectious laughter, as well as the way she pulled Kylie onto her lap and gave her a squeeze, made Toby think he'd better have a talk with his newly engaged brother.

There were a few questions he needed to ask Jude. Because maybe, just maybe, this funny and beautiful woman wasn't entirely off-limits after all.

Chapter Three

Ever since Angie had joined him and the kids for dinner on Saturday night, Toby hadn't been able to stop thinking about her. By Monday morning he was racking his brain, trying to come up with an excuse to see her—other than stopping by the Superette to pick up groceries, although he was tempted to do just that.

Then, while driving the kids to school, he had a lightbulb moment.

Brian, who was seated in front, was craning his neck and peering out the windshield at a plane flying overhead.

"Look at that one," he said, pointing it out to his younger brother, who sat in the back with Kylie. "Wouldn't it be cool to fly an airplane?"

And bingo! Toby had the perfect solution.

"How would you like to talk to a real pilot and see some planes up close?" he asked Brian.

The oldest boy had been unusually quiet and introspective since moving in with Toby, but when he glanced across the seat, his mouth dropped open and his eyes lit up in a way they'd never done before. "That would be awesome. Do you know one?"

"My cousin Sawyer and his wife, Laurel, own the new flight school and charter service. Laurel is actually the pilot. She was even in the air force."

"No kidding?" The boy's jaw dropped, and his eyes grew wide. "For *real?*"

Most people in town were more impressed with Toby's connection to the Fortune family, rather than the lovely woman one of his cousins had married. "Yes, for *real.* I'll give Sawyer a call this morning and ask for a tour."

"For all of us?" Justin asked.

"And for me, too?" Kylie chimed in. "If it's a girl pilot, I want to see her."

Toby laughed. "Yes, we'll all go. After I drop you guys off at school, I'll try to work out a good time for us to go. But no promises on when that might be."

And that was just what Toby did. Once the kids had gotten their backpacks, climbed out of the truck and headed for their respective classrooms, he called his cousin.

Sawyer's father, James Marshall Fortune, had been a triplet. His two sisters had been given up for adoption when they were very young. Josephine May was raised in England by the Chesterfields, a family that was both rich and royal. Jeanne Marie, Toby's mom, was raised in Horseback Hollow by loving parents who were common folk. But what they lacked in finances, they made up for in love.

Last year, Sawyer had met Laurel Redmond in Red Rock, where they fell in love. On New Year's Eve, they married in Horseback Hollow, where they now made their home. Sawyer and Laurel opened Redmond-Fortune Air, which served folks in this area. Laurel used to work with her brother, Tanner Redmond, who owned the Redmond Flight School and Charter Service back in Red Rock. They originally opened a branch of that company here, but with Tanner's blessing and Sawyer's capital, Laurel bought out her brother's stock and recently went out on her own.

When Sawyer answered the phone, Toby told him about Brian's interest in airplanes, then asked if he could bring the kids by the airfield sometime for a tour.

"Absolutely," Sawyer said. "Laurel flew a couple of businessmen from Vicker's Corners to Abilene this morning for a meeting, but she should be back before three."

"Is Angie Edwards working for you today?" Toby asked, as casually as he could.

"As a matter of fact, she comes in at one-thirty and will be here until four. Why?"

"No reason. I'd heard she was a part-time receptionist." Toby glanced at the clock on the dashboard, realizing he had a lot of chores to get done today. But no telling when Angie would be working at the flight school again.

"The kids get out of school at three," he told Sawyer. "So we'll head over to the airfield then."

And that was just what he did.

As had become his routine, Toby waited in front of the school when the bell rang. Only this time, he'd gone home so he could shower, shave and put on a new shirt and his favorite jeans.

"Did you talk to your cousin?" Brian asked, as he climbed into the truck.

"I sure did. And Sawyer said to come by today."

Whoops and cheers erupted from the backseat. Even the usually quiet Brian was beaming, confirming that Toby had just hit a home run.

So what if fulfilling a young boy's dreams to get to see the inside of a cockpit hadn't been his only motive? Besides, the kids had been talking about Angie nonstop—especially Kylie—and they were going to be just as excited to see her as he was. If he happened to talk to a beautiful woman and casually slip in a dinner invitation while they were at the airfield, then so be it.

"But let's set some ground rules," he told the kids. "You're going to have to mind your manners and not touch anything you're not supposed to. No running off—that means *you,* Justin. And the minute we get back to the ranch, you're going to have to sit down and do your homework. No complaints. Got it?"

A chorus of "got it"s and excited chatter filtered over the seat to him.

Fifteen minutes later, as the anticipation built in the cab of the truck, Toby turned down the county road that led to their destination.

Prior to the addition of Redmond-Fortune Air, the Horseback Hollow Airport hadn't amounted to much more than a small control tower, a couple of modular buildings, one of which housed Lone Star Avionics, several hangars and a relatively small airstrip.

But the brand-new building Sawyer and Laurel had built, with its gray block exterior, smoky glass windows and chrome trim, added some class to an otherwise small-town, nondescript airport that served both Horseback Hollow and nearby Vicker's Corners.

After parking next to Sawyer's new black Cadillac Escalade, Toby led the kids up the walkway and through the double glass doors into the reception area.

Angie, who was busy typing some letters at the reception desk, brightened when they came in. "Hey, look who's here!"

She greeted each child with a hug, but stopped short when she reached Toby. After all, what was required? Certainly not an embrace. And a handshake was much too formal.

They both settled for a smile, which worked out just fine.

"I heard you were coming." She turned to a guy in green coveralls who was seated near a potted ficus tree and reading a newspaper. "Pete, is Sawyer still out back?"

"Yep. He'll be in shortly." Pete lowered his newspaper and nodded at Toby. "How's it goin'?"

"Not bad."

Pete Nelson, a tall, lanky mechanic, worked for Lone Star Avionics and sometimes did side jobs for Sawyer and Laurel. Ever since Sawyer and Laurel opened up for business, the other employees at the airfield usually came over to use their break room, as well as the new fridge, microwave and coffeemaker.

"Taking a break?" Toby asked the thirtysomething air-force vet, trying to keep the hint of jealousy from his voice. After all, if he worked at the airfield, he'd be taking breaks in the office when Angie was here, too.

Hell, Toby didn't even work at the airfield, and he was looking for reasons to stop by the sexy brunette's places of employment.

"Just having a quick cup of coffee," Pete said. "Then it's back to the hangar."

"Hey, Justin," Brian said, as he wandered toward a table with a plastic-enclosed display of miniature-sized scale models of airplanes. "Look at this."

Kylie followed the boys, just as Sawyer entered the building.

"Hey, Toby." He extended his arm, and they shook hands. "Sorry I wasn't here when you arrived."

"No problem. We've been checking out the reception area." And the receptionist, who'd just bent over to reach into the lowest drawer of the filing cabinet.

Toby hadn't noticed before, but Angie was wearing a short black skirt. Well, it hadn't looked so short until she'd bent over and those long, tanned, shapely legs stretched out.

Wow.

Sawyer continued to talk, although Toby couldn't quite wrap his mind around what he was saying. Still, he nodded as if he'd heard every word.

When Kylie, who must have gotten bored looking at the miniature planes with her brothers, wandered over to Angie, Toby was about to call the little girl over to him and tell her that Angie was busy. But without missing a beat, Angie set her up at the desk with a stamp pad and paper, then went back to stooping and bending and flashing those long, shapely legs.

"Aw, so that's the way the wind is blowing," Sawyer said, calling Toby out.

"The *wind?*"

Sawyer lowered his voice to a whisper. "It's not the airplanes you're interested in. It's Little Miss Google. I'd wondered why you wanted to know if she was working today."

Toby tore his gaze from Angie, ran his fingers through his closely cropped hair and focused on Sawyer. "What are you talking about? Who's Little Miss Google?"

"Evangeline Edwards, our part-time receptionist and jack-of-all-trades."

Toby never had been good at lying, so he zeroed in on the subject he'd rather discuss. "Why do you call her Little Miss Google?"

"Because she's a walking version of the website. If you want any information about anything at all, there's a pretty good chance she knows it."

While Toby had never considered Angie to be dumb, she hadn't struck him as being exceptionally knowledgeable, either.

Had he missed something?

"You don't believe me? Watch this." Sawyer called across the open reception room. "Hey, Angie, Captain Schroder called a few minutes ago. Laurel wasn't around for me to ask, but he's flying his client's new Cessna Nav into Horseback Hollow. He wants to know how many feet per minute his descent should be."

Angie didn't look up from her work. "If his true airspeed is 75 knots, which is standard for most Cessna Navs on approach, our headwind component here is usually 15 knots. That would make his ground speed 60 knots, which you'd multiply by five for a rate of descent of 300 feet per minute."

"Thanks. I'll let him know." Sawyer gave Toby a little jab with his elbow, then tilted his head and lifted a single eyebrow as if to ask, *What'd I tell you?*

Toby had no way of knowing if what Angie had recited was true or not, but he figured it must be. Pete the mechanic hadn't argued the point. Of course, he still had his nose in the newspaper.

Moments later, Laurel Redmond Fortune came through the same back door Sawyer had entered. The lovely blonde greeted Toby with a hug, then gave her husband a kiss. "I'm going to grab a quick cup of coffee in the break room, then I'll give you guys that tour we promised."

"Take your time," Toby said.

As Laurel left the room, Pete lowered the newspaper he'd been reading. "Did you guys know that Herb Walker got busted for drunk-and-disorderly conduct last night outside the Two Moon Saloon?"

Sawyer gave Toby another little elbow jab, then said, "I wonder what kind of bail his wife will have to post for him."

"Normally, it would be twenty-five hundred dollars," Angie said, "but seeing how today is Monday and Judge Hanson doesn't approve of drinking on Sundays, drunk and disorderlies from the night before usually have to post four thousand."

Angie's position on her knees, as she placed the last

of the papers in the very back of the lowest drawer, gave Toby an excellent view of the rear end Doris Edwards had criticized days earlier. But Toby was so busy picking up his jaw off the floor that he was having trouble concentrating on those lovely curves.

How did she know those random facts?

When Sawyer and Pete started to laugh, Angie finally looked up and clued in to what was happening. "Were you guys doing that Google thing again?"

"What's a drunk and disorderly?" Kylie asked, reminding the adults that the kids were still hanging around.

"It's what Aunt Barbara got arrested for," Brian answered, displaying knowledge beyond his age.

The laughter suddenly ceased, and the adults sobered. Fortunately, Angie swooped in for the save. "Hey, Brian, Mr. Fortune said you could go sit in the cockpit of his brand-new Gulfstream. You can even touch every button and lever. And Mr. Nelson won't mind a bit putting them all back into place after you guys mess with them to your heart's content."

As a whoop went up from the kids, Angie cheekily smiled at her boss and the mechanic.

About that time, Laurel came out of the break room with her coffee. "Let's go, kids."

"I call first on talking on the headset to the people in the control tower," Justin said.

"I get to sit in the pilot's chair first," Brian countered, as he followed Laurel out the door.

"Wait for me," Kylie yelled as she tried to keep up with her brothers, who were already headed toward the hangar with Laurel.

The mechanic and Sawyer both gave Angie a look that promised they'd get even with her. But as far as Toby could see, they'd messed with Angie first.

It was nice to see that she gave back as good as she got.

"Laurel's going to need my help," Sawyer said.

"Mine, too." Pete set aside the newspaper, grabbed his disposable cup and followed Sawyer outside, leaving Toby and Angie alone.

Finally.

"How do you know so much?" he asked.

"I used to watch *Jeopardy!* a lot with my dad when he was sick, and trivial facts tend to stick in my brain. Plus, I did a lot of internet research when I was trying to decide upon a college major." She glanced at the clock on the wall, noting that it was four.

She straightened her desk, then shut down her computer. As she reached for her purse, she added, "Learning various oddball things is also a perk to changing jobs frequently. So I ended up knowing a little something about everything. Obviously, the flight stuff, I learned here."

As she pushed back her chair, he couldn't help noticing those long, tanned legs emerging from the skirt that no longer seemed too short.

"What about the drunk and disorderly?" he asked. "Is that from a job or from firsthand experience?" *Please don't let her be a party girl,* he found himself thinking.

"Do I look like the drunk-and-disorderly type?" She turned back to Toby. She must have noticed his gaze on her legs, because she crossed her arms and said, "Don't answer that."

"Sorry."

She didn't seem to be actually annoyed, though, because there was a spark of humor in her voice when she added, "Before that temp agency folded, they sent me to work at Señor Paco's Bail Bonds for a few weeks."

That was a relief. Not that he planned to actually date her.

Or did he?

"Aren't you going out with the kids to see the new plane?" she asked.

He'd much rather learn about Angie's control panel than some stupid airplane's, especially since it was four o'clock and she was leaving.

Who knew when he'd see her again, which brought out an unexpected sense of urgency, prompting him to blurt out, "Do you want to come over for dinner tonight?"

Dinner? At the Double H Ranch? With Toby and the kids?

The invitation had come out of the blue, and judging from the expression on Toby's face, Angie suspected that the question had surprised him as much as it had her.

"I'm not sure what we'll be having," he added. "I'll have to stop by the Superette and pick up something. But the kids need to eat tonight. And if you're not busy…"

"Actually, I have to stop by there to pick up my paycheck anyway. Do you want me to do the shopping for you?"

"That would be great." Toby reached into his back pocket, pulled out his wallet and peeled out a couple of bills. "Here's forty bucks. Pick up whatever you think the kids will like."

Great. The choice was hers, then?

Not only had she agreed to have dinner with him and the kids, she'd also agreed to plan the menu, which meant she'd be stuck trying to decide what to cook for a hungry man and three picky children.

What had she been thinking?

At least he'd given her the money to pay for the groceries. She wasn't sure how she would have been able to afford them if he hadn't.

"Do you know how to get to the ranch?" he asked.

She tossed him a smile. "I'm sure I can find my way there."

Ten minutes later, she was walking up and down the aisles of the Superette, grabbing packages and cans in record time.

Julia Tierney, who'd been working the check stand, laughed when Angie started laying items out on the conveyor belt.

"What's so funny?" Angie asked her friend and boss.

"Girl, I haven't seen you make such quick decisions on what to buy since that time you came running in here after that chili-pepper-eating contest with Mr. Murdock. You grabbed the first bottle of Mylanta you could find and drained it right in the middle of aisle three."

Sometimes, when Angie didn't have time to think about it, she could be rather decisive. And her tummy had been on fire that day.

She shook off Julia's teasing. "I'm picking up dinner for Toby and his kids this evening. And since I'm sure everyone's probably hungry, I don't have time to roam the aisles, stewing about what to cook."

Julia glanced at the items she rang up. "Pizza sauce, mozzarella cheese, pepperoni slices, mushrooms, ham, peppers, onions, ice cream, strawberries, instant bread mix. Looks like you'll be having homemade pizza."

"I figured it would be safe, especially if the kids can make their own."

"That's clever," Julia said. "I couldn't have come up with a better idea myself."

That was quite the compliment. Julia had always dreamed of going to culinary school or maybe getting a degree in restaurant management, but when her father suffered a heart attack, she'd decided to stick close to home and help out her parents with the store. So she'd given up her dream.

However, now that her father was better, it looked as though her dreams would finally come true. When Wendy and Marcos Mendoza finally opened up The Hollows Cantina in the next month or so, Julia was going to manage it.

"Yeah, well, I've learned that if you can't choose just one thing, it's best to have plenty of options available."

"Good idea," Julia said, as she totaled Angie's purchases.

"How are things going with the new restaurant?"

"Great. I love what Marcos and Wendy have envisioned, and it's really coming together. In fact, I was going over some of the job applications we've gotten and saw yours. We won't be scheduling interviews yet, but I wanted you to know that you're at the top of the pile."

"Thanks. That's nice to know." Angie helped Julia bag her purchases. "Who's going to take over for you here?"

"My mother's sister just retired from a cable-television company in Lubbock. So she's going to move in with my folks and help out for a while. I think it's all going to work out nicely."

"I'm glad to hear that."

"So tell me," Julia said. "This thing with Toby and the kids… That's a little intriguing."

Only because Julia was in love with Liam, Toby's brother. And she had stars in her eyes and thought everyone else should, too.

"We're just friends," Angie said.

Of course, she'd caught Toby staring at her legs a few times earlier today. And unlike a lot of other men she'd caught gawking like that, he'd seemed to be interested in more than just her appearance.

"Didn't I once hear you say that you never liked limiting your options?" Julia asked.

Yes, that was Angie. Her father had always told her that life wasn't an Etch A Sketch. That she ought to weigh each decision carefully, especially when it came to choosing a career—or a spouse.

Otherwise, she could find herself stuck in a really bad place.

She supposed that was why she'd never been able to settle on a college major or to find a job that interested her for very long—or a man worth making any kind of commitment to.

Angie didn't respond to Julia's question. Instead, she thanked Julia, took the two bags of groceries and headed for her car.

No, Toby Fortune Jones wasn't in the running when it came to considering romantic possibilities.

But if he wasn't an option, then what was he?

The answer came to her as she placed the pizza fixings into her car and prepared to head for the Double H Ranch.

Toby Fortune was one fine cowboy who was far too attractive for her own good.

Chapter Four

After Toby finished overseeing the homework hour, he told the kids they could watch television before dinner. Then he went into the kitchen to check the pantry. It wasn't as though his cupboards were bare. He could certainly rustle up something to add to whatever Angie planned to cook.

He'd no more than scanned the canned goods in the pantry when he heard a car pull up. Knowing it had to be her, he went outside to greet her.

As she climbed out of the driver's seat of a black Toyota Celica that had seen better years, let alone days, she reached into the back for the first of two eco-friendly bags. Her hair had been pulled back in a ponytail when she'd been at Redmond-Fortune Air, but it hung loose around her shoulders now—soft, glossy and teased by a light evening breeze.

She wasn't wearing anything different—just that black skirt and white blouse. Yet tonight, for some crazy reason, he found himself a wee bit... Hell, he didn't know what to call it—starstruck, stagestruck, dumbstruck...?

"Here. Let me help you with those." He reached for the bags, and she handed them over.

As they headed for the house, he said, "I'm sorry for not having stuff on hand to cook. When I lived by myself, I could go weeks without grocery shopping. But since the kids have been living here, it seems like I need to restock my fridge every other day."

She tossed him a carefree smile. "You should probably shop at one of those warehouse stores where you can buy in bulk and use a flatbed cart to haul your purchases to the checkout line."

"If I didn't have to drive clear to Lubbock to find one, I would. But then again, the kids wouldn't get to come into the Superette all the time and see you."

Toby chanced a glance at the woman walking next to him, wondering if she knew the kids weren't the only ones who'd miss seeing her.

"The kids are fun," she said. "I like it when they come in."

What if he didn't have children? Would she like it when he came in?

"Nice house," she said, as they entered the living room, which always managed to stay tidy because there wasn't a television set or a video game in sight. "I've always liked the ranch style."

Toby slowed his steps long enough to scan the white walls, the open-beamed ceilings, the distressed hardwood floors, the stone fireplace, as well as the leather furniture. "Thanks. I've been meaning to add a little color, maybe some Southwestern-style pictures on the wall, but I haven't gotten around to it yet."

"I'm sure the kids take up most of your free time."

"You got that right." He carried her purchases into the kitchen and placed the bags on the white tile countertop.

"What are we having?" he asked.

"Pizza. And just the way everyone likes it."

"Great idea. But I've never told you my pizza preference." There had to be some things even Ms. Google didn't know, unless she was psychic.

She tossed him a breezy smile. "I'll bet I even have your specific preference covered."

Something told him not to take her up on any wagers or else he'd end up in some wacky competition with her, just like Mr. Murdock.

But then again, Toby had always liked a good challenge. And Angie Edwards would prove to be one heck of one—if he were to pursue her.

"Hmm," she said, as she studied the directions on the box of instant bread-dough mix. "This might not be enough. Do you have any flour?"

"It's in the pantry. I'll get it. Is there anything else I can do to help?"

"You can wash the veggies, chop them up and put them in separate containers. Do you have a cutting board and knife?"

"Sure do."

While Toby got busy on his assignments, Angie began kneading the dough. Next they sliced the pepperoni and grated the cheese. Before long, they were moving around the kitchen seamlessly, almost as if they'd worked together a hundred times.

"So let me ask you something," Angie said.

Oh, no, here it comes, he thought. *She wants to know why I keep showing up at her workplaces and inviting her to hang out with me and the kids.*

"How do you do it?" she asked.

"Excuse me?"

"I couldn't help noticing your refrigerator door. It's plastered with papers—Kylie's artwork, Justin's B+ in spelling, the graph Brian created in math, not to mention that bulletin board with the YMCA flyers posted all over it. Then there's a list of dance classes and the schedule for swim lessons. I'm amazed that a single dad is so supportive of his kids. But what really blows me away is that LEGO-themed calendar you have on the wall."

"When I was a kid, our fridge was always covered in stuff like that. And my mom used to display all our awards and trophies throughout the house. She kept a bulletin board in the kitchen, too. Right next to the telephone. But why does the calendar surprise you?"

"Because almost every square this month is full. And just look at this list of YMCA classes. Nearly all of them are circled."

"You think that's too many?"

"Not for the kids. It's great for them. But the YMCA is in Vicker's Corners, which is a bit of a drive from the ranch. And I'm worried about you. I was an only child, with two parents. And it was all they could do to get me to school, the sitter and to any medical appointments."

"I have to admit, it's tough sometimes."

She crossed her arms, as if she was going to scold him, but she smiled and her eyes sparkled in mirth. "Toby, you're doing it to yourself. It's only April, and you have them in swim lessons? It's not even summer vacation yet."

"I know, but Justin can't swim. And he wants to go to camp in June. So I figured we'd better get started on those lessons so I won't have to worry about him." Toby shrugged and added, "Besides, I don't mind running them around. They've had it rough ever since their mom died. And they've missed out on a lot of things— like parents and a happy home. I just want them to see what it's like to have a normal family life."

"I think that's wonderful. So don't get me wrong. I'm happy for them. And I think it's awesome that you're providing them with so many opportunities, especially when you're the only one available to drive them back and forth. It's just that I know how much you must be sacrificing, and I'm not even talking about the cost of those activities."

Toby thought about the old beat-up car sitting in his driveway and the fixer-upper granny flat in which she lived. Apparently money was an issue for her.

He was pretty sure that Angie couldn't care less about his family's financial situation—or rather, the wealth most folks seemed to think they had by way of their rich relations. But he had reason to believe her mother didn't feel the same way.

So just in case he'd misread Angie, he figured it wouldn't hurt to let it be known that if a woman was looking for a wealthy "catch," she wouldn't find him living on the Double H Ranch.

"I want the kids to stay busy, even if that keeps me hopping. I hired a foreman early on to take on a lot of my work and responsibilities, which put another strain on the finances, especially since the Double H doesn't bring in that kind of money yet. So I've had to scrimp in other ways."

"Yes," she said. "I know."

He cocked his head slightly. So he'd been right? She was not only smart, but a psychic, too? No, that couldn't be right.

"What do you mean?" he asked.

She pointed to the bag of flour on the counter, which he'd picked up at the Superette because it was half the price of the name brand.

"Oh. You mean because I bargain-shop."

She laughed. "You didn't get a deal. That flour is too inferior for any proper baking, and it was aging on the shelf. So the price was discounted, but it still isn't selling—except to people who don't know anything about cooking."

"Oh, yeah? It seems to work well enough." Toby reached into the bag, grabbed a handful of flour and blew the mound directly into her pretty little upturned face. "See? It's light and airy."

"Oh, you…" Angie sputtered through the white dust covering her lower face, then quickly picked up a mushroom she'd been chopping and threw it directly between his eyes.

The vegetable struck him dead center. He laughed,

and she reached into the bag of flour—no doubt wanting to dust his face a ghostly white, just as hers was.

He grabbed her wrist to stop her, and she twisted, trying to pull free. Then, as their eyes met, she stopped. He stopped. For a moment, everything stopped—time, breathing, heartbeats....

No, not heartbeats. He could feel her pulse pounding in her wrist, under his fingertips.

Their gazes remained locked, and something passed between them. Before he could figure out just what the heck it was, Kylie ran into the kitchen, breaking the tension, as well as the silence.

When she spotted Angie, her eyes widened. "What happened to your face? It's a great big mess."

"I know." Angie laughed.

So did Toby. "She might be a champ at playing Ms. Pac-Man, but she's no match for Mr. Ranch-Man."

"Cute," Angie said. "Very cute."

He tossed her the dish towel closest to him. She caught it, then walked to the sink, dampened it and wiped off her face.

"Is dinner ready yet?" Kylie asked.

"Almost, honey." Angie grabbed a slice of Kylie's favorite American cheese. "Snack on this and I'll call you guys in just a couple of minutes."

"Okay." Kylie took the cheese, then dashed out of the kitchen and back to the family room.

Deciding to get their earlier conversation back on track, Toby said, "Actually, just to set the record straight, the Horseback Hollow Fortunes aren't rich like our cousins from Red Rock, Atlanta or the U.K. So taking on the kids did put me in a financial bind at first, but not for long. Someone apparently wanted to help out and donated money to cover those expenses and then some."

"That's amazing. What a generous gift."

"It certainly was. I wish I could thank them, but it was an anonymous donor."

"Could it have been their father or maybe one of their long-lost relatives?" she asked.

Toby snorted. "I doubt that. I'm more inclined to think that it was one of *my* long-lost family members."

"Who? Or would you rather not share that with me?"

"My best guess and number one suspect is James Marshall Fortune, Sawyer's father and my mother's brother. I think it was his way of indirectly giving my mom some of those shares of stock she returned to him last year. But I'm not going to push too hard to find out. If the donor wants to remain anonymous, then I'll respect that."

"Nevertheless, I still think it's wonderful that someone wanted to help the kids."

"That's how I see it, too. The money was actually given to me through an attorney in Lubbock, along with a note saying that it was to offset the costs I incurred by taking in the kids. But that I should spend it as I saw fit. That's what made me think the donor had to be my uncle." Toby raked his hand through his hair. "I wrestled with my pride for a while and was tempted to refuse it. But then I realized the kids really deserved it. And it would provide a better life for them. So I decided not to look a gift horse in the mouth."

"I assume it was a substantial amount."

"Enough to see them each through high school and

to pay for their college. So I put the money into a trust fund for them. It's invested and provides a monthly income that helps cover their expenses and pays for extra things like swim lessons and dance classes. Summer camp, too. Stuff like that."

"Wow. That's awesome." She tossed him a dazzling smile, then added, "*You're* awesome, Toby."

Angie gazed at him as if he'd just been awarded the Medal of Honor. And while he found her admiration touching, it also felt undeserved. So he lobbed a playful smile at her in return. "Yep. A horrible bargain shopper, but an awesome man."

Toby leaned toward the bag of cheap flour again and Angie threw up her arms in protection. "No, no, I give up. You are not only a good man, but a fine steward of your money. You make excellent shopping decisions. You should be on that coupon show on TV."

"Now I know you're full of it," Toby said, laughing along with her.

Teasing had been a way of life in the Fortune Jones household, and he liked that Angie was the kind of woman who found it so easy to banter.

"Okay," she said. "The ingredients are all set."

"Do you want me to call in the kids?"

"Go right ahead. I'll turn on the oven and get the drinks." Angie went to the refrigerator door, paused and stared at the most recent flyer. "Speaking of saving money, it looks like they're offering two free weeks of classes at the Y this month. Maybe I should check into that. I've always wanted to see what yoga is all about."

Toby didn't know if she was talking to him or to

herself, but apparently there was yet another interest she wanted to add to what had to be a lengthy list.

She tossed him a pretty smile. "Who knows? Maybe I'll become a yoga instructor someday."

"Speaking of people who run around too much," he said, returning her smile with a teasing grin, "what about you?"

"Me?" Angie tilted her head slightly and furrowed her brow. "What about me?"

"You seem to change jobs a lot. Why not find a good, full-time position and stick with it?"

"I will someday. But I want something that I can feel passionate about. Maybe, if I keep trying different things, I'll eventually find the career I'm best suited for."

He hoped she came across it soon—for her sake.

And maybe for his. She really was easy to talk to, and the kids adored her. If she were more settled, he'd like to see where this relationship—if he could even call it that—would go.

But he couldn't risk allowing himself or the kids to get too close to someone who could be gone working on an oil rig or joining the military or going to cosmetology school or wherever the wind took her next month.

Unless, of course, Angie had already worked on an oil rig and had crossed that off her to-do list.

If he didn't have the kids and didn't need her help, he'd...

He'd what? Cut her loose?

That might be the wisest thing to do.

So why did he feel like reeling her in?

Because she was beautiful. And fun to be around. In fact, if he didn't have the kids to think about, good ole dependable Toby might even consider doing something wild and crazy—like having a one-night stand or a weekend fling with her.

Talk about something totally out of character for a guy like him.

But yeah, if he were footloose and fancy-free, that was exactly what he'd do.

As he took another glance at Angie, saw the glimmer in her eyes, caught a whiff of her citrusy scent...

Well, heck. If he had a babysitter willing to spend the weekend at the ranch with the kids, he just might consider taking Angie for a night or two on the town in Lubbock anyway.

The pizza-making station had been a smashing success. Altogether, they'd created three medium lopsided pizzas, one supersized with only meat, and one that was perfectly formed with every single topping.

Once the homemade creations came out of the oven, the kids could hardly wait for them to cool before they scarfed them down.

"Thanks for dinner," Toby said. "It was awesome."

"It sure was," Justin said. "I never made pizza before. It was fun."

"I'm glad you liked it." Angie turned to the boys. "Hey, guys. I don't suppose I could get you to do me a favor. After we get the kitchen cleaned up, I was hoping you'd teach me a few tricks on your PlayStation. I need a crash course."

"Sure!" Justin turned to his older brother, and the boys pumped their fists in the air.

"Seriously? You want a lesson from the kids?" Toby asked. "And why the big rush?"

"Mr. Murdock won his grandson's PlayStation from him in a poker game."

Toby lifted his eyebrow. "He gambled with a kid?"

"Long story. Anyway, he's been beating me left and right on Madden."

"Oh, great," Toby said, a spark of humor in his tone. "I thought I'd brought in adult reinforcement, but I've ended up with a fourth kid."

"Come on," Justin said. "Let's go, Angie."

"We have dishes to do first," she reminded him.

"No, you go ahead," Toby said. "I'll take care of the cleanup."

"Are you sure you don't mind?"

"After you pulled off such a successful dinner? Heck no. Besides, I'd hate to see Mr. Murdock get the best of you again."

She laughed, then took off with the boys.

Twenty minutes later, Toby reminded them that it was a school night.

"Aw, man," Justin said.

Angie wrapped her arms around his shoulders and gave him a squeeze. "You heard what Toby said. Maybe I'll come back another night, and we'll play again."

Toby let the kids stay up long enough to eat a bowl of ice cream topped with fresh strawberries for dessert. Then it was time for them to go to bed.

Overall, it was one of the best evenings Angie had ever had. At least since... Well, since she'd had dinner with Toby and the kids a couple of nights ago at The Grill.

Kylie approached the chair where Angie was sitting and placed a hand on her knee. "Will you read my Disney princess book to me before I go to bed?"

"I don't mind." Angie looked at Toby for the ultimate okay.

"It's all right with me. Each night at bedtime, I read a story to her. After that, I read a chapter out of *Treasure Island* with the boys. We're at a pretty exciting part, so it'll be nice to get back to where we left off."

What a nice family ritual. Angie was glad she'd been given a chance to take part in it.

By the time she'd read the princess story twice, gotten Kylie two glasses of water to drink and checked in the closet and under the bed for dragons three times, Kylie finally drifted off to sleep.

As Angie quietly sneaked out of the little girl's room, she wondered if she should wait for Toby, or just let herself out. Fortunately, she didn't have to make a decision.

Having finished his bedtime duties, Toby was already back in the living room, picking up ice-cream dishes and putting the sofa cushions and throw pillows back in place.

"Listen," he said, "I can't thank you enough for your help with the kids. When I do handle bedtime by myself, it takes another hour."

"The kids really are amazing." And Angie meant that from the bottom of her heart. She couldn't believe her mom had referred to those sweet, adorable children as "rug rats."

"Look at *you,*" Toby said. "You're the one who's *amazing.* I can't believe how quickly the kids have taken to you. Brian even talked to you about the girls in his class, and Justin didn't try to sneak off to the barn once while you were here. And Kylie… Well, I can't even tell you how great it's been for her to be around a woman. My mom and my sisters help out whenever they can, but they've got such full schedules and lives."

Did he think Angie didn't have much of a life? Or was she reading too much into what he was saying?

"Anyway," he said, "you're great with kids. Are you planning to have some of your own someday?"

"I haven't really given it much thought." She'd never been around children all that much. And her mom hadn't made any big deal about motherhood— or parenthood, for that matter. So she'd never really considered it one way or the other.

She did have to admit, though, that being around Toby's kids had made her see motherhood in a brand-new light.

"I suppose I'd have to think about getting married first," she said. "And that's never been a priority."

Toby seemed to straighten at that. "You mean to tell me that you're twenty-four, incredibly beautiful, fun and smarter than an internet search engine, and there hasn't been a single guy who's come along and made you think about bridal showers and wedding cakes and the whole nine yards?"

Toby thought she was beautiful? And fun? And smart?

"I…uh…thought about it once, but it didn't work out." She hoped he wouldn't ask for details. She hated talking about it. And there'd been so many witnesses that inevitably the subject always seemed to crop up when she least wanted it to.

"What happened?" he asked.

So much for hoping.

"I dated this guy once. David. He wasn't especially handsome, but he was bright and had a great personality. I really liked him, so we dated a couple of months—which was longer than most of my relationships last. But one night, he ruined everything."

"What did he do?"

"He insisted upon taking me to the Two Moon Saloon, and when we arrived, a lot of my friends were there. Even my mom showed up, which should have been a major clue that something was off-kilter. But apparently, come to find out, my mother had been coaching him."

"Your mom *coached* him? What happened?"

"Apparently, with her help and encouragement, David planned this elaborate and romantic proposal in front of an audience. Everyone was expecting me to say yes. So I did. And then two days later, I gave him the ring back."

"Why didn't you want to marry him?"

"Everyone asked me that same question. The truth is, I didn't know. And I still don't. Heck, I can't even commit to a brand of shampoo long enough to take advantage of a two-for-one sale. How could I have made a lifelong commitment like that without feeling something?"

"You didn't feel anything for him? I thought you said he was a great guy."

"Yes, but I never had the zing. You know what I mean?"

"I'm not sure that I do."

"It's that heart-spinning, soul-stirring rush that you get when you know the other person is 'the one.'"

"I can't say that I've ever felt that way," he said.

"Yeah, well, I've never felt it, either. But I've read about it. And if I ever make that kind of forever-commitment to someone, I want to feel it. And I didn't have it with David."

"So you broke up with him."

"Um. Yeah. But I should have ended things way before I did." She blew out a sigh.

Toby didn't say anything. He just stared at her. But she knew what he must be thinking. It was the same thing everyone else always thought about her—that she was unreliable and scattered and wouldn't know a good decision if it fell from the top shelf of a Superette display case and landed straight on her head.

Suddenly embarrassed that she'd revealed so much, she realized she'd better regroup, which was her standard operating procedure when things got sticky or icky or whatever.

So she grabbed her purse and decided to bolt before she could change her mind, climb into Toby's lap and tell him that she was already feeling more for him than she'd ever felt for David.

And before he could respond by reiterating that he wasn't looking for a girlfriend or a potential mom for his foster kids.

"Anyway," she said, "I have to get home before it gets too late or I'll have Mr. Murdock out looking for me."

"Thanks again for dinner."

"You're more than welcome. I'll see you around town sometime."

She was just about to make her escape when he tossed her a smile that sent her heart spinning and set off a little…?

Oh, no. It couldn't be.

Surely, it wasn't.

But it certainly felt like a zing.

Chapter Five

Angie had been kicking herself the past two days for bolting from Toby's house the other night. He'd never even commented on her story about David, yet assuming he'd think the worst of her, she'd left before he could say anything.

Wasn't that typical? When the going got tough, Angie skedaddled.

But why had she been in such a hurry to escape? If he hadn't considered her to be flighty before, he probably did now.

She just hoped she hadn't ruined their friendship, because she really enjoyed her time spent with him and the kids. She was just about to close down the register and clock out when the subject of her thoughts for the past forty-eight hours approached with the kids in tow.

"We're getting ice cream," Kylie announced, as she placed a frozen chocolate bar on the conveyor belt.

"I thought an after-school treat was in order," Toby said.

If he'd wanted to avoid her, he could have stopped by The Grill for that ice cream. So obviously he hadn't thought that badly about her.

"What're you guys up to today?" she asked, as she rang up his purchase.

"I need to take Justin to the YMCA for his swim lesson," Toby said. "But Kylie's dance practice was moved up earlier in the day, which is a problem since I can't be in two places at once. And so, I wondered if there was any chance you'd be getting off soon."

"As a matter of fact, I am."

"I don't suppose you could do me a huge favor."

When he gazed at her with those big baby blues, she said, "Sure."

Anything, she thought.

"Can you either take Kylie to dance or Justin to the Y?" he asked.

"Actually, I'd planned to stop by the Y and check out that yoga class today. So I can take Justin with me, then bring him to the ranch when we're done."

"Great. That would sure help me out. And this time, I'll have dinner ready for you."

"Meals at the ranch could become habit-forming," she said.

"Maybe, but everything seems to go better when you're around." He flashed her a smile, and there it went.

An almost definite zing.

Twenty minutes later, Angie dropped Justin off with his swim instructor, a lanky teen who barely looked old enough to drive. She wondered if he was qualified to be giving lessons and certified in CPR, but she decided he must be or the Y wouldn't have hired him.

"I'm going to take my class now," she told Justin. "You'll probably get finished a few minutes before me, so change into your dry clothes, then meet me by the vending machines. I'll buy you a candy bar as soon as I get there."

"Cool."

She remembered Toby telling her that the eight-year-old wasn't a very strong swimmer, so she wanted to make sure that he didn't hang around the pool without supervision. He also had a habit of wandering, so she figured a bribe to stay at a designated location was a good idea.

Satisfied that Justin was in good hands—and that she'd thought of everything, Angie headed to the front desk to find out where the yoga class was being held.

A young woman, clearly the receptionist, pointed her down the hall.

Angie turned in that direction, her gaze scanning the entry of the building, just as Mr. Murdock pushed open the double doors and walked inside.

He was wearing a red T-shirt with Semper Fi printed in yellow letters in front. He also had on a pair of green-and-white Hawaiian-print swim trunks and blue flip-flops.

"Hey," she said. "What are you doing here, Mr. Murdock? Are you a member of the Y?"

"Just joined yesterday. My doctor says I gotta exercise. So I'm heading out to the aquatics area. Thought I'd swim a few laps. How about you?"

"I just dropped off Justin, Toby's boy, for his swim lesson. And while he's there, I'm going to take a yoga class. They're offering free classes this month."

"You and Toby are getting pretty tight," Mr. Murdock said, lifting a single gray brow in that paternal way of his.

"We're just friends. I've been helping out with the kids."

"Humph." Mr. Murdock folded his arms and rested them on his ample belly. "Is that what you call it?"

Okay, so she'd been questioning that herself, too. But she wasn't about to admit it—especially in public.

"No need for you to be jealous, Mr. Murdock." She gave the old man a wink. "My heart will always belong to you."

"Glad to hear that, Girly. I'm getting pretty used to having you around the house." Then he winked back at her and shuffled off toward the pool, leaving her to scope out that yoga class—which she'd better hurry to or she'd be late.

When the class was over and she'd released her last pose, Angie didn't stick around to talk to anyone. Instead she hurried to meet Justin and buy him that treat.

But when she reached the vending machines, he was nowhere in sight. Were there other places to get snacks in the building that she hadn't known about? Some that were outside?

Oh, no. Not by the pool. She'd tried to tempt him with a treat to keep him away from the water.

She quickly made her way out to the aquatics area,

which was directly behind the building. But after a quick scan, she still didn't see him.

Darn it. Where was he? She should have known better than to have taken that yoga class. She should have sat by the pool and watched his swim lesson instead.

Panic set in, raising her heart rate to the level of a full-scale cardio workout. She hurried into the building, but she didn't dare ask if anyone had seen him.

What if word got out that she'd lost him? Not only would that further perpetuate everyone's belief that she was unreliable, but social services might get wind of it. What if they investigated Toby and somehow found him lacking because he'd entrusted a child with a flaky, irresponsible friend?

Mere seconds later, both of those concerns paled when she still hadn't found Justin. Where could he be?

When she spotted the swim instructor coming out of the men's locker room, she nearly accosted him when she asked, "Have you seen Justin Hemings?"

"No, not since his lesson ended ten minutes ago."

Oh, God. He could have been kidnapped, whisked away from here by some predator. And all on her watch.

Angie rushed back to the aquatics area for one last look, the teenage instructor now fast on her heels.

The area had pretty much cleared, except for Mr. Murdock, who sat on the edge of the pool's shallow end, his feet dangling into the water, his face red, his breathing labored, his hand clutching his chest.

Oh, dear God. Poor Mr. Murdock was having a heart attack. What else could possibly go wrong?

"Call 911," she told the swim instructor. "That man needs an ambulance."

Then she ran to her friend to let him know that help was on the way. When she reached him, he pointed to the pool, where Justin's body lay at the bottom.

"No!" she screamed, as she leaped into the water, clothes and all. She grabbed the child, pulled him to the surface and dragged him to the steps. "I've got you, honey. I've got you."

Justin, whose eyes opened and grew wide, appeared dazed. Or was he confused? He looked at Mr. Murdock, gasped, then called out, "What was my time? Did I win?"

"Win?" Angie shrieked. "Win what?"

"Me and Mr. Murdock were having a contest to see who could hold their breath the longest."

In her panic to save the boy's life, Angie had nearly forgotten about Mr. Murdock. But several bystanders, as well as YMCA employees, had now gathered around the older man and were trying to help.

"Are you okay?" one woman who appeared to be in management asked the retired marine.

"The paramedics are on their way," the teenage swim instructor said.

"You won...that round," Mr. Murdock told Justin, his voice coming out in short little pants. "But give me...a second. We'll go...best two...out of three."

A *contest?* They'd been having a fool competition?

Angie, who'd always prided herself on being cool, calm and collected in a crisis, practically shouted, "*Nobody* is going back in that water. You two nearly scared the living daylights out of me. And the whole time you were only competing in a stupid challenge. I can't blame Justin for acting childish. But really, Mr. Murdock, you should know better."

Before the elderly man could respond or even catch his breath, the ambulance arrived, along with a hook-and-ladder truck. Two firemen brought a gurney to the pool, while a female paramedic carried her bag and placed it next to Mr. Murdock.

The tough old man waved her away, especially when she tried to attach an oxygen mask to his face.

Justin seemed none the worse for wear, thank goodness.

"Can I have a ride in the ambulance?" he asked one of the firemen.

"That depends," the fireman said, nodding toward Mr. Murdock. "Is this man your grandfather? And did you ride with him here today?"

"No, they're not related," Angie clarified. "And we're *not* riding in the ambulance. We need to go back to the ranch."

"Then can I see how you turn on the siren?" the boy asked.

"Maybe after we get this gentleman loaded up," the fireman said.

"Who, *me?*" Mr. Murdock asked, apparently realizing that the 911 call had been made for him. "I ain't going nowhere in no damn ambulance. And I don't need no siren. My ticker is just fine. I only got a little winded after a friendly competition with the boy."

"A competition?" the paramedic asked. "Maybe we should start at the beginning. What's going on here?"

Justin explained what had happened, going so far

as to tell them how Angie had tried to save his life, even though it didn't need saving.

"Mr. Murdock beat me the first round," Justin said, "but he taught me how to let the bubbles out my nose to keep the air in my lungs longer."

"Well, I don't think Mr. Murdock's lungs are doing so great right about now," Angie mumbled in frustration. Her worry now switched to the old man.

Mr. Murdock finally ripped the oxygen mask out of the female paramedic's well-intentioned hand and threw it about ten feet into the pool.

Then he pointed an arthritic finger at the poor woman only trying to do her job. "I *said* I don't need medical attention. What I need is a Scotch and a cigarette."

Angie wanted to tell the old man that she didn't think his lungs could take the extra stress of inhaling tobacco right this second. But before she could, he turned to her and said, "You done good, Girly. No one was drowning, but if the kid had been, your response time was the quickest I've ever seen."

A wet Mr. Murdock in a saggy bathing suit shuffled to his feet and dripped his way to the changing rooms with the paramedics still following him.

A 911 call was big news and everyone inside the YMCA had now gathered around the pool area to watch. There was no getting around it. She was going to be the talk of the town before nightfall.

Angie, her yoga outfit drenched in water and stuck tight to her skin, pulled Justin into her lap and held him close. Thank God everything had turned out okay.

Still, as she glanced at the oxygen mask floating to

the deep end of the pool, she sighed. What a day. She might have had the best of intentions, but she'd really screwed up.

How was she ever going to tell Toby that she'd nearly lost Justin—and that she just might be as flighty and irresponsible as everyone seemed to think that she was?

Toby had just pulled the chicken off his outdoor grill when the headlights of Angie's Toyota flashed, letting him know she was turning up the drive that led to his house.

He'd put Brian in charge of making the salad with the promise that if the kid could master assembling some easy dishes in the kitchen, Toby would teach him how to man the grill next time.

And it had worked like a charm.

When Angie and Justin climbed from the car, Toby called out, "You guys are just in time for dinner."

Neither of them spoke as they slowly made their way to the patio at the side of the house.

That seemed a bit odd.

Toby flashed Angie a smile, which she didn't return. And that was his second clue that something had gone wrong.

Why was her hair all wet and slicked back?

Uh-oh. Her clothes were wet, too.

Before he could ask, she said, "We had a bit of an incident at the pool."

"What happened?"

When she didn't give him a speedy reply, Justin answered. "Me and Mr. Murdock were having a breath-holding contest, and Angie thought I was drowning. So she jumped in the pool to save me."

Justin glanced at Angie, then at Toby, his eyes wary as though he was bracing himself for a scolding. But Toby was still waiting for Angie to say something.

Apparently, thinking he was off the hook, Justin brightened and really opened up. "It was pretty sweet, though. The firemen and paramedics came—with sirens and everything. But best of all, I beat Mr. Murdock at holding my breath. And then he cussed. And Angie yelled at both of us. And even though the fireman said I couldn't ride in the ambulance, but I could look inside, Angie wouldn't let me. But that's okay, because—"

Toby interrupted the boy's rambling dialogue and said, "Kiddo, why don't you go get some dry clothes on before dinner. I'll let Angie tell me the rest of the story."

There was no telling what all had transpired at the YMCA earlier, but knowing Justin's history of wandering off and Mr. Murdock's fierce competitive streak, Toby was able to piece a lot of it together.

After Justin ran inside, Toby turned his full attention to the soaking-wet woman. She'd better get out of her clothes, too.

Whoops. Now that was an intriguing thought. And an arousing one, seeing how the Lycra now covered her like a sexy layer of skin. But as tears filled her eyes, his thoughts cooled to sympathy.

Justin said she'd been angry earlier, but she appeared to be hurt now. Crushed, actually.

Uh-oh. This was bad.

What in blazes had happened?

"I'm *so* sorry," she said. "It's all my fault. I shouldn't have gone to that yoga class. I should've just stayed out by the pool with him. And then, when he wasn't where he was supposed to meet me, I thought of all the terrible things that could have happened to him, and I panicked. I guess you could say I had a meltdown, and everyone saw the whole thing."

"It couldn't have been that bad," he said.

"Oh, no? If I'd been on an E.R. reality show, the TV ratings would have shot through the roof. It was terrible, and I completely lost it."

She started rambling then, just as Justin had. And while her sweet face still looked confused in the aftermath of her unnecessary panic attack, the snug workout pants sent his testosterone soaring, and he nearly dropped the platter of grilled chicken he was holding.

Damn. If he didn't have his hands full, he'd pull her to him, wet Lycra and all, just to offer his comfort and whatever else he could.

"Salad's ready!" Brian yelled out the side door. "I'm starved. Can we start eating?"

"You go ahead and eat with the kids," Angie told him. "I'm not hungry. I need to go home and get out of these wet clothes. If you want to talk more about it, we can do that in the morning."

Then she turned toward her car.

"Wait!" Toby called to her back.

When she turned around, he said, "I'll give you some dry clothes and a glass of wine. You look like you could use both. And after dinner, you and I can sit down and enjoy some quiet time—adults only. Then you can tell me what happened. Or, if you'd rather, you can forget all about it."

Whatever would make her smile again.

That was, unless she wanted to get the hell away from him and the kids as fast as her toned legs would carry her.

And quite frankly, he wouldn't blame her if she did. After all, he'd known all along how it would end. And he'd implied as much to her a few days ago when they'd discussed his nonexistent love life.

Women saw him as some sort of Captain Rescue at first. And then they ran for the hills as soon as they came face-to-face with the reality of dealing with three kids, each of whom still had some issues after living in a dysfunctional household with their aunt Barbara. But they seemed to be getting through all that, especially since Angie had started coming around.

"You know," she said, "a glass of wine sounds great. Besides, if I go home now and run into Mr. Murdock, I just might ring his little ole leatherneck."

Toby laughed. At least her sense of humor was coming back.

He shifted the plate into his left hand, then slipped his arm around her shoulders. She leaned into him, and he gave her a gentle squeeze.

A guy could get used to comforting her, even when she was soaking wet. In fact, Toby might have just stood there, holding her all night, except he had children to feed.

"Come on," he said, as he led her to the kitchen, where the kids had gathered.

Once inside, he assigned them all chores so they

could eat sooner. "Check the rice steamer, Brian. Kylie, set a place for Angie. She's staying for dinner."

Kylie, who was down on her hands and knees, looked up from the floor, where she was picking up some dropped silverware. "I already set the table. Well, all but the forks and spoons."

Toby was about to warn her to get fresh utensils from the drawer, then he figured he may as well forget it since the housekeeper had been here today and had mopped the floor. So at least for tonight, the three-second rule for germ-free drops had become a three-minute rule, as far as he was concerned.

While the kids did as they'd been asked, Toby took Angie to his bedroom, where he began opening drawers, looking for something she could wear, something that might fit.

When he caught her looking at the king-sized bed in the center of the room, he wondered if she was thinking the same thing he was.

And just what *was* he thinking?

Right now, he didn't dare put it into words. Instead, he haphazardly handed her a worn-out Houston Texans T-shirt, along with a pair of his old cross-country shorts from Horseback Hollow High, which he figured would be too big.

If he had his way, he'd prefer to see her stay in those tight pants and sports tank. But they were wet. And even if they were dry, he had to find something else for her to wear—and quick.

It was killing him to see her looking so sexy and so vulnerable at the same time, especially since she was just an arm's distance and mere steps away from his bed.

"While you change," he said, "I'll get the wine."

Minutes later, everyone was sitting in their places when Angie came to the table. The kids must have picked up on her solemn mood, because they were so quiet you could hear a pin drop—or a man's heart beat, his blood race.

She'd rolled his shorts up at the waist to make them fit her. The shirt barely reached the hem of the shorts, making it look as though she wasn't wearing anything underneath.

Man, he needed to get a grip. There were kids present.

And thankfully, the kids soon began to chatter, because Angie remained quiet through dinner, sipping her wine and picking at her food.

When everyone else had eaten their fill, Toby said, "Okay, guys, no TV tonight. It's already time to pick up your rooms, take your baths and get ready for bed."

It really wasn't all that late, but Toby had waited long enough to get Angie alone.

With her being as pensive as she'd been at dinner, he hadn't expected her to help out with the evening routine the way she'd done the other night she'd been here. But she surprised him by stepping right up to the plate, which was nice. The kids liked having her around.

He did, too. But he'd have to be careful that nobody got too attached. Especially him.

When Toby finished reading the next chapter of *Treasure Island,* Angie was still with Kylie, so he went to the kitchen and started to clean up. He'd just loaded the dishwasher when she entered the room, her shoulders slumped.

"Come on," he said, wiping his hands on a dish towel. "The rest of this can wait until tomorrow."

After refilling her wineglass, he grabbed a cold beer out of the fridge for himself. Then they walked into the living room. The house was noticeably quieter with all the kids tucked in.

She took a sip of the chardonnay before practically collapsing on the sofa. He recognized the signs of an adrenaline dump. Or maybe she was just emotionally exhausted.

He sat next to her, and it seemed only natural to reach out, to touch her shoulder, to finger her hair. "Okay, tell me what's bothering you."

She let out a ragged sigh. "I feel as though I've let you down."

"Why would you think that? The way I see it, you took your responsibility seriously. I'm actually impressed."

"Thank you, but I never should have let him out of my sight in the first place." She closed her eyes.

"Don't blame yourself. The same thing happens to me at least four times a week. Justin is impulsive. He has a history of running off and doing his own thing, which led to some of the behavioral problems he was having at school. We've been working on correcting it, but he's eight. It happens. I should have better prepared you."

She shuddered, and he adjusted his body so he could pull her even closer. He reminded himself that she was upset and vulnerable now, but she felt so good in his arms. He stroked her back, his fingers unhampered by any bra straps. And with those long, tanned legs bare to her thighs, she was practically naked.

Aw, man. It would be so easy to take advantage of the situation. But should he?

Then what?

She had her head cradled against his shoulder, and he was tempted to kiss the top of her head—a gentle kiss meant to comfort. But something told him he wouldn't want to stop at gentle.

Or at the top of her head.

And kissing her would take their relationship to a level neither of them was ready for, not when three kids stood in the balance.

So he reined in his lust and didn't kiss her at all. But he probably should have taken the opportunity while he'd had the chance, because it seemed as though she was pulling away from him and getting to her feet before he knew it.

She was leaving? So soon?

"It's been a long day," she said. "I need to go."

He followed her to the door. He hated to see her go, but the fact that she was wearing his shirt and shorts gave him some comfort. If he wouldn't be sleeping with her, maybe his clothes would.

"Thanks for dinner and for understanding," she said, as she grabbed the oversized purse and the wet shoes she'd left just outside the front door.

When she straightened, their eyes met.

A good-night kiss crossed his mind, but he pondered the wisdom of doing so for a beat too long, because she said, "I'll talk to you later."

Then she headed for her car.

As he stood on the porch and watched her go, the sway of her hips and those long, shapely legs taunted him. He kicked himself for his lack of courage, his foresight and his strong sense of family values—or whatever the hell had convinced him to do the right thing and keep his lips and his hands to himself.

He'd had two opportunities to kiss Angie tonight, neither of which he'd taken. He tried to tell himself that he'd done the right thing, that he'd made the right call, but his libido wasn't buying it.

But wouldn't you know it? Once he'd lost his chance to kiss her, he wanted her all that much more.

Chapter Six

After Angie left, Toby went into the bathroom to take a shower and spotted her wet workout clothes hanging over his towel bar. He'd assumed she'd taken them with her, along with her purse and the wet shoes she'd left outside by the door, but apparently, she'd forgotten them after she'd changed.

He'd return them, of course, which would give him an opportunity to see her again soon.

That was a good thing, right?

Less than twenty minutes ago, he'd been tempted to kiss her. In fact, he'd been tempted to do more than that, right there on his living-room sofa—and despite having a house full of kids.

But that *wouldn't* have been good. He blew out a sigh.

As long as those three children were depending

upon him, he'd better not even think about having a woman spend the night. And since he hoped they'd be living with him until they each went off to college, he'd better get used to sleeping alone—unless he tied a cowbell around each of their necks.

The image of him doing that was actually kind of funny, and he might have even chuckled out loud if being twenty-six and facing the possibility of ten years of near celibacy wasn't downright unsettling—and unthinkable.

Surely it wouldn't come to that.

He ran his hand through his hair, then turned on the water in the shower, adjusting the temperature to warm—hoping cold sprays wouldn't be the only ones in his future.

Something told him this was going to be a long night, and that sleep would be a long time coming.

And he'd been right.

The next day, as soon as school let out, he surprised the kids by driving to the Superette and telling them they could each pick out a snack. As they unbuckled their seat belts, he reached for the plastic bag holding Angie's now-dry workout clothes.

Then he herded the happy kids into the mom-and-pop grocery store, riding pretty high in the saddle himself. No matter what he told himself, being with Angie always brightened his day.

Trouble was, once he got inside and the kids took off, he didn't see her at any of the checkout registers.

Where was she? He could've sworn that she worked at the market on Thursdays. But it was tough keeping up with her schedule. Had he been wrong? Was she working for Sawyer and Laurel today?

Dang. Was this what his life would be like if he were to actually date her? Would she always be working at some odd job, changing shifts frequently, possibly moving to another city?

She didn't have a history of stability, and no matter how many family conversations she livened up or how many heated looks passed between the two of them, nothing was going to change that fact.

Just when he began to realize he'd have to take the plastic bag back to his truck, Justin ran up and asked, "Can I have one of Angie's cupcakes? She put little race cars on top and everything."

"Slow down, Justin. What are you talking about?"

"I'll show you." The boy turned and dashed off toward the bakery section.

Toby followed him to the display case—and to Angie, who stood behind it, wearing a white apron tied around her slim waist.

"See?" Justin said, imploring Toby to tear his gaze from Angie and to look at the tray of cupcakes behind the glass enclosure, each one blue and topped with candy sprinkles and a tiny toy race car.

"You're a baker, too?" Toby asked her.

"It's a long story. The baker called in sick, so I stepped in. And when I spotted the toy cars stashed in one of the cupboards in back, I thought they might add a little more pizzazz. Apparently, the customers agreed because we sold the first batch already and the second is going fast."

"So can I have one for my treat?" Justin asked again.

"I want the one with the purple car," Kylie chimed in.

"All right," Toby said. "We'll take 'em."

"Do you want to eat them here?" Angie asked. "Or should I box them up for you?"

Justin, always one for instant gratification, said, "I want to eat mine right now."

Toby laughed. "I'll never hear the end of it if I make them wait."

Angie carried the cupcakes to one of the two small bistro-style tables, where the morning customers enjoyed their doughnuts and coffees. She set them before Justin and Kylie, then passed out a couple of napkins, just as Brian walked up with a highly caffeinated energy drink in his hand.

"I'm gonna just have this instead of a snack," Brian said, as he sat down at the table.

"Oh, no, you won't." Toby snatched the can out of the boy's hand. "Kids aren't supposed to drink this crap. It's not good for you."

"Mike Waddell drinks it all the time at school," Brian argued.

"Maybe so," Angie said, as she set a cupcake in front of the boy. "But Mike Waddell got detention last week for jumping out of his seat seven times during that movie in science class. He also had eight cavities at his last dentist appointment."

As the kids dug into their cupcakes, Toby followed Angie behind the bakery display case and lowered his voice. "How did you know that about Mike Waddell?"

"We live in a small town, Toby. People talk. Especially Brian's teacher, Mrs. Dawson, and Wendy Cummings, the dental hygienist." Angie glanced at the plastic bag he still held. "What's that?"

"The clothes you left in my bathroom." He handed them to her.

She flushed, then scanned the area as if they were making a drug deal and she didn't want to get caught. Then she stashed the bag in one of the drawers near the cash register.

Was she embarrassed? Whatever for? It wasn't as though she'd spent the night at the ranch and left her panties behind, although the thought of her doing that made him smile.

She lowered her voice. "And that's another thing people have been talking about and why I'm really back here in bakery and not out in front."

Because people thought she and Toby were...sleeping together?

"What are you talking about?" he asked.

"Several people who came through the checkout line asked me about the incident at the pool. They'd heard from a neighbor, who'd heard from a cousin, who... Well, you know how small towns are."

Yes, he did. And there wasn't much he could do to stop a rumor like that from getting out. But heck, if he was going to be the subject of gossip, it was too bad he couldn't have had a night to remember it by.

"Finally, around ten this morning, I asked Mrs. Tierney if she could man the cash register for a while," Angie said. "And so she let me work back here instead."

"All because of a little misunderstanding?" Toby shook his head. "That reminds me, though. How is Mr. Murdock?"

"He was here this morning, having coffee and holding court. He gave everyone a firsthand account of what happened. He…uh…also mentioned to Mrs. Rhodes, who was on her way to The Cuttery for her shampoo and set, that I've been helping you out a lot with the kids."

Should that be a secret? Toby wondered. Apparently Angie thought so because the pink flush on her cheeks deepened.

"Actually," he said, "you've been a godsend. And I really appreciate your help more than you can imagine."

"Even after yesterday?" she asked.

He laughed. "I told you before. I've had my share of bad days, too. It happens."

Angie glanced at the kids, who'd finished their cupcakes and were now racing their frosting-coated cars along the table, then looked at Toby and smiled. "To be honest, I've really enjoyed helping you, too. The kids are great, and I'm actually surprised at how much I like spending time with them."

What about their foster dad? Toby wanted to ask. *Do you enjoy spending time with him, too?*

But he knew better than to let things get personal, especially when he really did need another favor from her tomorrow. Besides, he'd picked up on what she'd left unsaid earlier.

If Mrs. Rhodes knew Angie was spending so much time with him and the kids, it wouldn't be long before all the other women getting their hair done at The Cuttery would start linking him and Angie romantically.

He really didn't mind what people said, but he didn't think Angie would like it, especially if her mom got wind of it. Doris Edwards had been pushing Angie to find a husband. And if the eligible men in town thought she was already taken, it might ruin her chance of going out with a guy who could offer her more than a cattle ranch and three foster kids.

Although the thought of her going out on a real date with someone else reared up inside of him, throwing him to the ground like an unexpected buck from a mild-mannered horse.

Maybe, in that case, he ought to keep her unavailable for a while—until he figured out where this thing was going. Or where he wanted it to go.

"I feel bad asking you this," he said, "but I'm in a bind. I'd ask Stacey, but she works and has her hands full with Piper."

"I'd be glad to help," Angie said. "What do you need me to do?"

"I have a meeting in Lubbock tomorrow afternoon, and I'm not sure when I'll get back. Is there any chance you could pick the kids up from school and take them home?"

"I have a few things to do, but it shouldn't be too hard to reschedule them. Let me work on that. In the meantime, don't worry about the kids. I'll pick them up from school. And I'll have dinner ready for you when you get home."

Well, what do you know?

He was back in the saddle again.

The meeting in Lubbock had gone later than Toby had expected, so he called Angie before he left town and told her to go ahead and feed the kids.

"Don't wait for me," he said.

"We're having spaghetti," she told him. "I'll keep a plate warm for you."

"Sounds good. Thanks."

"Did your meeting go well?" she asked.

"It sure did. I've been negotiating a deal on a piece of property that backs mine, and the man who owned it had refused to sell. But he passed away last spring, and his widow doesn't want to deal with it any longer. Her late husband thought it was a lot more valuable than it really is, so we had to agree upon a price."

"Great. We'll have to celebrate when you get home."

"Sounds good to me."

"Oh," she said. "I hope you don't mind, but I told the kids they could have a movie night after dinner."

"That's fine. I'll see you in a bit."

When the line disconnected, he turned on the radio, letting Gladys Knight fill the cab with her soulful voice as she sang about a midnight train to Georgia.

See, all you Texas country music fans. Willie Nelson isn't the only one who can sing about the Peach State.

The song had barely ended when his cell rang.

Toby glanced at the lit display, but didn't recognize the area code. Still, he turned down the volume on the radio, took the call and pushed the speakerphone button. "Hello?"

"It's Barbara Hemings, Toby."

The kids' aunt. He glanced in the rearview mirror, then pulled to the shoulder of the road and let the truck idle.

"Hi, Barbara." He wanted to ask her how rehab was going, but the woman sometimes became defensive, so he let it be. Besides, he had a feeling this wasn't going to be a social call, which was why he wanted to have his hands free in case he needed to make any notes about something she said.

"I heard about what happened at the pool the other day, so I put in a call to the case worker from child services. I'm waiting for her call back, but I thought you should know that just because I'm stuck in court-ordered treatment, I haven't stopped fighting for my kids."

They weren't *her* kids. And she'd had a lot of opportunities to fight for them, especially when she had custody, but she kept blowing it. However, arguing with her wasn't going to solve anything.

"I'm not sure where you're getting your information, Barbara, but that incident was blown all out of proportion. Justin was never in danger at the pool. The kids are all safe, and they're happy. And just so you know, I've already called Ms. Fisk and given her a heads-up about the situation. I'm sure she'll tell you the same thing when she calls you back."

"Toby, you're a young, single man with a tumbling-down ranch. And those kids can be a handful at times. There's no way you can handle them on your own."

Tumbling-down ranch? He'd turned the Double H around in the three years he'd owned it. And, thanks to the meeting he'd had thirty minutes ago, he'd be running more cattle next year, and that meant he'd be turning an even better profit—if things went according to plan.

"As I seem to remember," he reminded her, "you were single when you took the kids on, too. And my 'tumbling-down' ranch is a hell of a lot nicer than that cockroach-infested motel you had them living in when the state took them away from you."

"Yes, and that turned out badly. But I'm better now."

At least the woman was able to admit the obvious.

"Anyway," she added, "the kids need to be with family. And if they can't be with me for the next few months, then I want them with one of my relatives."

What family? If there were any Hemings relatives nearby, wouldn't they have stepped up by now?

"Do the kids even know these relatives?" Toby finally asked, his fingers gripping the steering wheel until his knuckles ached.

"No, but they're family, Toby. You of all people should understand about long-lost family."

She was talking about James Marshall Fortune coming to Horseback Hollow and finding his sister, Jeanne Marie, Toby's mom. Although, quite frankly, Toby was surprised that she even knew about that.

"I have a cousin in California," Barbara said. "I'm going to ask him to take the children until I get out of rehab."

Great. Another upheaval? And just who was her cousin?

"What's his name? What does he do?"

"His name is Rocky, and he's looking for work. His parole agent thinks he can find a job by the end of this month. His wife works at a hospital out there, but one of his conditions of parole is that he's not allowed to work at hospitals anymore, so that's out. But there are plenty of other places where he can get work."

His parole agent? He couldn't work in a hospital

anymore? If the cousin couldn't be trusted in a hospital then he sure as shooting couldn't be trusted with Brian, Justin and Kylie.

What made Barbara think that the children would be better off with some deadbeat cousin they didn't even know than they would be with Toby?

"I don't think that's in the children's best interest, Barbara."

"Honestly, Toby, it's not your decision. I thought you'd be a little more cooperative, but I guess the kids can't count on you for that."

The woman disconnected the call before Toby could throw the phone out his open window, which was what he'd wanted to do the moment he'd heard her voice.

He sucked the country air into his lungs and counted to ten, the way his pitching coach had taught him to do when he'd been on the mound.

Think. Whom did he call first? Ms. Fisk, the case worker? Or an attorney?

He glanced at the clock on the dashboard. Crap. It was too late to call anyone today. That would have to wait until tomorrow. He continued to sit in the idling truck for a while, his hands on the steering wheel, his thoughts on the troubling call.

Would the court decide that the kids were better off with a sketchy family member over a stable and caring guardian? It didn't seem feasible, but then again, anything was possible…

He did his best to shake off Barbara's threat, telling himself he didn't have time to worry about that blasted woman. He'd told Angie that he was going to be late, but he hadn't meant to completely abandon her with the kids.

After checking for traffic, Toby pulled back onto the road and accelerated.

At times like this it was nice to know he had someone to rely on, especially Angie.

People might think that she was flighty—and they might even be right. But either way, she was proving to be a real blessing.

A man could get used to going home to a woman like her.

Angie sure hoped Toby got home soon, because she was fading fast. She hadn't slept very well the past two nights, thanks in large part to the residual stress and worry from that 911 fiasco at the Y.

Even her mother had heard all about it and called, asking her what had happened. Sheesh. What a pain that conversation had been.

But at least Toby trusted her enough to ask her to help with the kids again.

It hadn't been easy to adjust her schedule to accommodate his, but she had. She'd worked a split shift at the Superette, going in early this morning. Then she'd left at ten o'clock to take Mr. Murdock to his doctor's appointment in Vicker's Corners. After that, she'd run over to Redmond-Fortune Air to type some letters for Sawyer. And it was back to the Superette for another two-hour shift, after which she purchased the ingredients she needed to make spaghetti for dinner.

She was nearly late picking the kids up from school, but she got there just in the nick of time. Then it was a quick stop at her house for the surprise she'd planned for the evening.

A couple of summers ago, she'd worked at an old movie theater outside of Lubbock. When the Red Raider Cinemas went out of business, the owner gave Angie a projector and several old movie reels. She'd always wanted to have an old-fashioned movie night under the stars, but she'd never gotten around to planning one. That was, until tonight.

Too bad she was about to nod off from exhaustion. She could really use one of those energy drinks Brian had wanted yesterday afternoon.

Hopefully, Toby would be home soon. He'd told her not to wait dinner for him, and they hadn't. At this rate, she was going to start the movie without him, too. Otherwise, she'd probably curl up on his sofa and nod off before he even got home.

She'd fixed him a plate and left it on the stove. Then she'd cleaned up the kitchen. She'd made popcorn, but had to make it the old-fashioned way, since Toby didn't have any kind of popper. She'd just salted a large bowl for them to share when Brian came in.

"We're all done," he said. "Me and Justin hung up the white sheet, just like you told us. And Kylie made beds for us on the lawn. You ought to see it."

Angie followed the boys out of the house, where they'd set up the makeshift outdoor movie theater. And, just as Brian had said, Kylie had, indeed, made them a giant bed—with every blanket, sheet and pillow she could possibly find.

"Did you leave any of the beds made up in the house?" Angie asked her.

"Nope," Kylie said. "Even Toby's blankets and pillows are out here."

That wasn't quite what Angie had in mind, which meant there was going to be a big mess to clean up afterward, when she doubted she'd have the energy to deal with it. But she wasn't about to scold the kids when the whole idea had been hers in the first place— and when they'd tried so hard to follow her instructions.

Besides, look how happy they were.

"Okay," she said. "Let's get this show on the road."

She'd just finished setting up the projector with the *Star Wars* film threaded in the proper slots, when Toby's Dodge rolled into the driveway.

"What's all this?" Toby asked, as he stepped out of his truck.

"Movie night!" Justin yelled, as he barged out of the back door in his pajamas and dived onto the bedding on the lawn, calling his spot.

Toby looked nearly as tired as Angie felt—probably realizing they'd have four beds to make up before anyone could go to sleep tonight.

Angie hoped she hadn't blown it by throwing the impromptu cinema party in his backyard.

Toby nodded to the old projector. "Where in the world did you get that thing? Wait, don't tell me. Does it have something to do with an old job?"

His grin and a glimmer in his eye teased her in a way that didn't make her feel quite so bad about her history of random employment. But she sidestepped his question and asked one of her own. "You look tired. Would you rather we do this another night?"

"And disappoint the kids?" Toby's grin blossomed into a smile, easing her mind. "No way. Let me get out of these clothes and put on something more comfortable."

Angie had been so busy reading into Toby's expression, which hadn't matched the upbeat tone of his voice when he'd called her earlier, that she'd failed to notice that he wasn't wearing his trademark jeans, T-shirt and cowboy boots.

He was dressed in black slacks, a button-down shirt and expensive dress boots. He looked sharp— and ready for a night on the town without the kids.

She wondered what it might be like to actually go out on a date with him—if they had a sitter.

That was, if he'd actually ask her to be his date.

As Toby headed into the house, Brian and Kylie followed Justin's lead, rushing outside in their pajamas and choosing their own spots to spread out on the blankets.

But Angie's thoughts were on Toby.

"I'll get the popcorn," she told the kids. "Showtime is in five minutes."

She made her way into the house slowly. She didn't want Toby to think that she was following him.

But what if he'd wanted her to?

Oh, get a grip. She was so sleep-deprived, she was becoming delusional.

She was about to carry the first load of refreshments outside when Toby stepped into the kitchen.

"Thanks," he said, his eyes contradicting the simplicity of his single word as they bored deeply into her own.

She tried to downplay the intensity in his gaze, as well as her efforts to provide a fun evening for the kids. "It was no big deal."

"Actually, it's a big deal to me. You have no idea how much I need this right now."

She thought Toby was going to pull her in for a hug, and she would have willingly gone—if he'd made the first move. But as her heartbeats pounded off the seconds and he didn't make the attempt, she realized it was probably more likely that one of the kids would come flying in the door to ask what was holding them up.

So she handed him the bowl of popcorn and grabbed the five ice-cream-filled mugs by their handles and led the way out the back door.

"So what are we watching?" Toby asked as he settled into the only spot the kids had left open, which happened to be right beside Angie.

"Star Wars I," Justin said.

"No, dude, this is *Star Wars IV,*" Brian said snarkily, as if Justin was an idiot.

"How can it be number IV when this is the first *Star Wars* they ever made?" Justin challenged back.

Angie quickly explained the nuances of the *Star Wars* episodes before the boys came to blows across the blankets.

"So you're both right," she said.

The boys conceded, going back to their ice cream.

"Is that my bedsheet?" Toby asked as he studied the improvised movie screen nailed to the side of his barn.

"Well, the boys' sheets are dark blue, and Kylie's has a *My Little Pony* print," Angie defended.

"Why is there a big brown spot on it?" Toby asked, glossing over the fact that the boys had put nail holes into his sheet.

"Justin dropped his end in some manure while I was on the ladder trying to nail it in place," Brian explained.

"I'm sorry," Angie said. "I didn't know they were going to use real nails. And I didn't realize they'd dropped it in cow… Well, in…you know. I just thought you had stained sheets."

Toby looked at her as if she'd been the one to drop the manure outside the barn in the first place.

"Did you try the popcorn yet?" she asked, trying to get the conversation heading in a different direction. "I put extra butter on it for you."

Toby reached into the bowl. "That stain on the sheet makes it look like Luke Skywalker has melanoma on his face."

"What's 'melanoma'?" Brian asked.

"It's a kind of skin cancer," Angie answered.

The pillows looked so comfortable. Maybe she could just put her head down for a second and rest her eyes, maybe even doze off for a moment or two.

"My mommy died of cancer," Justin said.

"Is Luke Skywalker gonna die of cancer, too?" Kylie asked.

Oh, no. Angie hadn't meant to mention the C-word.

"Nobody is going to die tonight," Toby said, trying to save the day.

But that didn't make Angie feel much better. If her brain hadn't been so sleep-deprived, she might have thought before opening her mouth.

Here she was, trying to do something fun and nice for the family, but then she'd screwed everything up by reminding them of their dead mother.

No matter what she tried to do, it seemed that she only made things worse. Maybe Toby and the kids would be better if she ran for the hills and stayed out of their lives forever.

They'd be better off. But as she scanned the yard, taking in the sweet kids and the handsome cowboy who'd taken them in and given them a home, she wondered how she'd ever just walk away from them without looking back.

Or did she dare risk it all and stick around until she finally got things right?

Chapter Seven

The kids settled back on the blankets to watch the movie. Toby and Angie did, too, stretching out next to each other.

By the time Han Solo was telling Leia that he was in it for the money, Toby leaned over and whispered to Angie, "Is there any more popcorn?"

He hadn't eaten lunch, so he'd pretty much wolfed down the spaghetti Angie had set out for him, but it really hadn't quite filled him up.

"I'll run in and make some more," she said, getting to her feet.

He hadn't meant to put her to work. "You don't have to do that."

"Actually, I was about to fall asleep. It'll help me stay awake."

Toby followed her into the kitchen. She may not

need any help, but he saw an opportunity and decided to take it. With the kids so engrossed in the movie, he didn't know when they'd get another chance to be alone. And the longer he'd lain next to her, the more he'd craved some one-on-one adult time with her.

When she realized he'd followed her into the kitchen, she said, "I'm so sorry about bringing up the C-word earlier."

"Don't even give it another thought. Everyone slips up now and then. Besides, I was the one who brought up melanoma in the first place. And if it makes you feel better, the social worker told me that the kids need to talk about their mom. It's better for them to process her death in a normal, healthy way. When they lived with their aunt, they saw a bad example of hiding emotions behind the bottle."

Just thinking about Barbara reminded him of the unsettling conversation they'd had. He'd almost forgotten about it once he'd gotten home. Angie had a way of getting his mind off his trouble, which was one more thing he liked about her.

Should he tell her about the call?

He didn't consider the idea very long. He didn't want to dump any more on her than he had to, no matter how easy she was to talk to. She wasn't in this thing for the long haul anyway.

Besides, why did he want to think about Barbara when he had Angie in front of him now, standing at the stove, heating oil and popcorn kernels in a covered skillet?

When the corn began popping against the lid, she

moved the pan across the burner—back and forth, faster and faster—her breasts swaying with the motion.

Aw, man. If he didn't stop gaping at the mesmerizing sight, those kernels wouldn't be the only thing popping.

"Is the popcorn done yet?" Justin yelled from the open doorway.

If you were talking about being hot and bothered, Toby was certainly close to done.

"Just about," Angie called out to the boy. "I'll bring it out to you in just a minute."

Justin ran back to the movie, and Toby decided he'd better do the same before his thoughts got the better of him.

A few minutes later, Angie joined them in the yard, bringing the replenished bowl with her and settling back into her spot next to Toby. Even the action scenes, with swishing lightsabers, zooming X-wing fighters and intergalactic battles, didn't keep Toby from wanting to reach out and grab more than a handful of popcorn.

But he managed self-control.

By the time the credits started to roll, he looked over and saw that Kylie and Justin had fallen asleep.

"I guess we'll have to carry them in to bed," he whispered to Angie, who'd nuzzled into the pillow next to his.

But she didn't answer.

He leaned over and, while tempted to brush back the strands of hair that had fallen across her face and tell her the movie was over, he let her sleep.

Brian, thank goodness, picked up his blankets and

pillow and made his way into the house on his own. But Toby had to carry the smaller kids one at a time.

Thanks to Kylie's overzealous efforts to make them all cozy for the movie, the mattresses were completely bare. Remaking all the beds seemed like way too much work to do. So instead, he went back to the grass, retrieved a couple of blankets and put one over each of the sleeping children.

When he returned outside and saw Angie curled up under the stars, the corner of his comforter tucked under her chin, he stood there and watched her for a while.

Now what? Wake her up? Send her home?

Invite her inside?

He looked back at the house. Considering the bare mattress that awaited him inside, he figured, what the heck.

She looked so soft, so comfortable. Why not let her nap? He could certainly use a little snooze himself.

So he lay down next to her, just as they'd done when the movie had first begun. Then he pulled a blanket over the top of them. Surely one of them would wake up in an hour or so. At that time, they could each go their own way, she to her house and he to his own room.

And no one would be the wiser.

Toby might not be able to invite Angie to actually spend the night in his bed, but this seemed like the next best thing.

Angie wiggled backward, not quite ready to wake up from her dream.

When had her bed gotten so small and cramped?

Her back was pressed up against a warm wall, her bottom nestled against something hard.

Her waist was tethered down.

She didn't feel trapped or claustrophobic, though. Nor did she feel compelled to move away. Rather, she snuggled deeper into the cocoon of comfort.

Whatever had been clamped on her waist slowly traveled upward until it reached under her shirt and began to fondle her breast.

Ooh. Nice. She sighed and arched in contentment, her dream getting better by the minute.

A warm breeze whispered along her neck, as lips brushed against the sensitive skin below her ear.

She leaned her head back to provide more access to the mouth that was giving her such delicious pleasure.

Swish.

Swack.

Swish.

What was that flapping sound?

Angie didn't want to stir, didn't want to ever wake up, but the annoying sound wouldn't go away. She cracked her eyes open and saw something big and white floating up in the wind, then smacking down against the side of a huge, red barn.

A barn that looked a lot like Toby's.

Why was her bed in Toby's backyard?

Wait. Whose pink-pony-covered pillow was wrapped in her arms?

And whose hand held her left breast? Whose fingers had tightened over her taut nipple?

"You feel good," a sleep-graveled, baritone voice whispered against her ear.

Toby?

This wasn't a dream, was it?

Swish. Swish. Splat.

Were those water droplets that just sprinkled her face?

"What the—" Toby shot up, and his hand left her breast. "Oh, hell. The sprinkler."

Angie stared at Toby through wet lashes, fully awake now and trying to piece together why they'd been sleeping together outdoors, why he'd been holding her so intimately. But more water from a nearby sprinkler shot her in the face again, and Toby grabbed her arm, pulling her toward the house.

"We have to get this stuff inside. Everything's going to get soaked."

Angie, still dazed from her erotic sleep-induced bliss, didn't take the time to decide whether Toby had been fully awake or dreaming. Instead she snapped out of it long enough to run for the movie projector, pull the hefty old machine off the relocated patio table and lug it, extension cord and all, inside the kitchen, trying to dodge the shooting sprays of water as she went.

She set the reels on the table, just as Toby dropped the first load of wet blankets on the kitchen floor.

"Why are you guys all wet?" Kylie asked, walking into the kitchen before Angie could process what had happened outside on the lawn.

Angie waited for Toby to answer because she didn't think the words would form in her throat.

But a red flush on Toby's face as he reached down for one of the damp pillows and placed it in front of his waist suggested that her hormones hadn't been the only ones getting an early-morning workout.

She didn't know whether to laugh at his discomfort or run out of the room in embarrassment because, whatever had just happened—sleep-induced or fully conscious—their friendship had just taken a tremendous turn in an unexpected direction.

Maybe it was best if she got out of here.

She was usually good with smooth exit strategies, but she couldn't seem to get her brain to engage.

As much as she'd like to pretend this morning hadn't happened, she hated to leave Toby to face the music alone. And judging from the pink tint blossoming underneath his stubble-covered cheeks, he didn't quite know what to make of it, either.

"The sprinklers came on early this morning," Toby mumbled, not dropping the pillow. "So Angie and I were trying to get all this stuff inside."

"Why didn't you bring it in last night?" Justin asked, making his way into the crowded kitchen, oblivious to the strong but awkward sexual attraction swirling in the room like a Texas dust cloud.

"Sweet," Brian said, padding in to join them, his red hair sticking up on one side of his head. "You guys had a sleepover."

Oh, great. That wasn't going to look good in the social worker's report—if one of the kids happened to mention Toby having a woman spend the night while the kids were home.

Angie reached up to smooth her own sleep-tousled hair.

Maybe she should tell the kids she'd been out for a morning jog and had decided to stop in for breakfast.

She glanced down at her bare feet. No, they were

too smart to fall for that. She needed to nip this thing in the bud before everyone in town heard that she and Toby had slept together—which, technically, they had.

"It wasn't really a sleepover," she said. "I just dozed off while watching the movie."

"Then can Mike Waddell kinda fall asleep over here next Saturday after our baseball game?" Brian asked.

The energy-drink kid? Angie could only imagine the hyperactivity that would come along with that night. But at least the focus was now off her.

"We'll talk about it later," Toby said, finally releasing the pillow.

"If Brian gets a sleepover, then can I have a slumber party?" Kylie asked.

"How many girls do you want to come to your slumber party?" Angie asked.

"My teacher said that, if we have a party, we have to invite everyone from the class so we don't hurt anyone's feelings. And we have twenty-three kids in our class. But I don't want to invite Destiny Simmons because she told everyone my hair looks funny because I don't have a mommy to do it right."

That reminded Angie that Kylie needed a real mother figure, someone permanent. And not a fly-by-night female role model who'd nearly made love to a man outdoors in broad daylight, with three impressionable kids inside the house.

"Twenty-three kids?" Toby asked. "But that's counting the boys, too. You can't invite them to a girls' slumber party."

Kylie pointed at Angie. "But *you* had a *girl* over for a slumber party."

The tiny red-haired cherub in the princess pajamas had brought the conversation full circle without missing a beat.

And just as quickly, Toby opened the pantry door and changed the topic. "Hey, guys. We need to get our chores done early today. Why don't I make pancakes for breakfast? You can help me by setting the table and getting the juice out of the fridge."

Smart move. New focus.

While the children were distracted with setting the table and getting the orange juice out of the refrigerator, Angie decided it was the perfect time to sneak out of here.

She was such a coward. But she was doing what she did best—leaving before things got uncomfortable again.

So she slipped out the back, quietly shutting the door. When she walked by the kitchen window, Toby spotted her and lifted his eyebrows.

She gestured, then mouthed, "I have to go." It was a lame excuse, especially since she really had nowhere to go on a Saturday morning. But she couldn't very well stay here and play house with Toby and the kids.

He nodded as if he understood. Yet guilt, embarrassment, fear and other emotions she hadn't yet pegged all tumbled around in her throat, threatening to cut off her air supply.

She put her thumb to her ear and her pinkie to her lips, giving him the universal sign for telephone. Then she mouthed, "I'll call you."

Again, he nodded.

Then she climbed into her car before she could debate whether she really had any business calling Toby at all.

Ten minutes after Angie drove away, the cordless phone on the counter rang and Kylie answered it before Toby could make a grab for it. Was Angie calling him already? He could understand her wanting to get the heck out of Dodge this morning. He'd been tempted to jump in her car and go with her just to escape the curious eyes pelting him with unspoken questions.

What had he been thinking, spending the entire night with Angie like that? Better yet, what had he been thinking setting those damn sprinklers on a timer to go off at six in the morning? If they hadn't blasted them with water, Toby knew exactly what he would have done to Angie's sweet, warm and tempting body this morning. He wouldn't have stopped with a hand on her lush breast—that was for sure. Instead, they'd gotten sprayed with water like a couple of dogs someone had to turn the hose on to keep from going at it on the front lawn.

"Yeah, Aunt Stacey," Kylie said. "He's right here, fixing pancakes for us and Angie."

Obviously, Kylie still hadn't realized that Angie had left. Or that Toby was still staring out the kitchen window after her like a sad, abandoned puppy.

He tried to reach for the telephone before Kylie could tell his sister anything else, but his hands were full of slimy eggshells, which he'd have to rinse off first.

"Uh-huh," Kylie continued. "Angie and Toby had a

sleepover last night. And Toby got my pillow all wet, but that's okay because he said I get to invite my class over for a slumber party."

With his hands clean, but still wet, Toby took the phone from Kylie. "Hey, Stace. What's up?"

"Why did Kylie put *you* on the phone?" Stacey asked. "I wanted to talk to Angie."

"She's not here," Toby said, a bit more defensively than he'd intended.

"She left already?" Justin asked. "Aw, man. I wanted to ask her to help me build a spaceship out of LEGO."

"We'll see her later," Toby told the disappointed boy.

But the truth was, he didn't know when they'd see Angie again. Or if Angie would even want to see him after the way he'd been pawing at her this morning.

"Later, huh?" Stacey asked. "I heard the two of you have been spending a lot of time together lately, but I had no idea you guys were at the sleepover stage."

Toby covered the mouthpiece. "Brian, stir the pancake mix. I'm going to talk to my sister for a sec. But don't use the stove until I get back."

After giving all the kids an assignment, Toby walked into the living room so they wouldn't hear his line of defense.

Not that he'd done anything wrong. Had he? Maybe if he just explained what had happened…

Hey, wait. He didn't owe anyone an explanation.

When he reached the living room, he asked, "So how's Piper?"

Everyone knew Stacey adored her nine-month-old daughter, so he figured he'd change the subject to one of toothless grins and sleepless nights.

"She's fine," Stacey said. "Growing cuter and smarter every day."

"And how about Colton?" he asked, hoping he could get her talking about her new fiancé, one of the neighboring ranchers. "Have you guys set a date yet?"

"Colton is doing great, but don't try those distraction tactics on me. I'm one step ahead of you, big brother. You are *not* getting out of this one. What's going on with you and Angie Edwards?"

His sisters, Stacey and Delaney, were protective over all their brothers, but particularly Toby since his family always accused him of being a softy—and a sucker for a sob story. Not that Angie was a sob story.

"Nothing's going on," he said. "Angie's been helping me out with the kids. That's all."

"Are you paying her for babysitting services? Because I heard Angie's always looking for a new job. She never seems to stick with one very long."

"Not that it's any of your business, but no, I'm not paying her. She's doing it to be nice and because she likes the kids. And for your information, Angie is a very hard worker. Just because she hasn't found a career she likes doesn't mean she isn't a good person."

"I never said she wasn't, Toby. I was just telling you what I've been hearing around town. I went to high school with Angie, remember? She used to date a lot back then."

Toby felt a jostle of jealousy stir up again in his veins.

"What do you mean she used to date a lot? Like she was…" Toby didn't want to say anything that would be demeaning to Angie, but he didn't know how else to ask.

"Well, she didn't have a reputation for being fast or anything like that, but she was known as the Queen of the First Date."

"What does that mean?"

"It means she would go out with a guy if he asked her, but usually, they never made it to a second date. I don't know if it was fear of commitment or what, but she never went steady with anyone or took any of the guys seriously. She for sure never had sleepovers with anyone before. Or at least none that I heard about."

The envy died down a little bit inside him. At least he couldn't fault Angie for being choosy.

"Listen, last night wasn't a sleepover. It was just an accident. Nothing, uh, really happened."

He hoped his sister hadn't caught the hesitation in his voice.

"Aha!" she said. "Define 'nothing.' And 'really.'"

"I'm not defining anything." Toby looked back to the kitchen to make sure none of the little ears had made their way within hearing distance.

Stacey clicked her tongue. "You wouldn't be getting so defensive if your relationship was strictly platonic. So how far have you guys gone?"

Toby couldn't believe Stacey had just asked him that. "This isn't high school, Stace. We're not playing truth or dare. I'm not talking about my sex life with my little sister."

"So you're saying there *is* a sex life to talk about," she said, a spark of excitement lighting her voice as if she'd tricked a leprechaun into revealing the location of his pot of gold.

Embarrassment was an understatement. Toby remembered holding the wet pillow up to cover his arousal this morning when the kids came into the kitchen. He wished he had something to hide behind now.

He wasn't going to admit to anything. He'd said too much as it was and figured silence was his only option.

"So," Stacey said, apparently changing tactics, "the reason I called was to tell you that Mom and Dad are having a family dinner at their house tonight. And we'd like you to bring Angie."

"Why, so you guys can check her out and pump her for information? No way."

"Mom told me and Delaney you'd say that when we came up with the idea."

Great. His family was already plotting and scheming.

"That's why," Stacey continued, "Delaney is calling Angie right now and asking her to come over for dinner. Too bad she didn't pick up the phone a few minutes earlier. We could've killed two birds with one stone."

"I'm not coming to dinner tonight," Toby said. "And I'm not inviting Angie."

"Why not? If there's nothing going on between you two, then why try to keep her away from your family?"

Stacey had a point. Unfortunately, with the sparks that were jumping between him and Angie lately, he doubted a blind man would believe there wasn't anything going on between them.

And knowing his family the way he did, he was

sure they'd figure out something was up the second he, Angie and the kids walked in the door.

Hell.

"Okay," he finally conceded. "But let me invite her. And I'll only do it if you guys promise not to interrogate her."

"My, aren't you the protector. She's lucky to have you in her corner."

Toby didn't know about that.

"Oops," Stacey said, "Piper just smeared green beans all over herself. Gotta go."

Good, Toby thought. He was glad Stacey's baby had made a mess she'd have to clean up. That was what his sister got for butting into Toby's business.

He just hoped he didn't have an even bigger mess to deal with now.

Angie saw Toby's name displayed on her caller-ID screen. She'd been too chicken to call him after she said she would. What was the proper length of time one should wait to call the man they'd intimately nestled against all night long? Three days? Maybe there was an article in some women's magazine she could reference.

Ugh. She needed to get this over with. He was probably calling to tell her that they needed to see less of each other. That he wasn't looking for a relationship. He'd made that more than clear. The sooner she bit the bullet, the sooner she could get over him. Unfortunately, she didn't think she'd ever get over the feeling of his fingers stroking their way up her waist. Or his husky voice telling her how good she felt.

She tried to sound more upbeat than the groan stuck in her throat would allow when she said, "Hello?"

"Um, hey."

Couldn't he even manage a proper greeting? He must already be experiencing remorse at what they'd done and guilt over what he was about to tell her.

She should make it easy for him and call things off first, but she couldn't bring herself to say the words for him.

"Did my sister Delaney call you yet?" he finally got out.

"Not that I know of. But I haven't looked at my missed calls since I got out of the shower."

Why would Delaney be calling her? Had the rumors started already? Was Toby trying to do damage control? Maybe they needed to get their stories straight about her spending the night out at the Double H.

"Good. I wanted to talk to you before she did."

Uh-oh. This didn't bode well.

"It sounds like my family is doing a dinner thing tonight and they want me to bring you."

"Why would they want me there?" Unless they thought something was going on between her and Toby. Of course, she didn't know why his family would think that when she, herself, had no idea if there was anything going on between the two of them.

"They, uh, well, they're just curious about you since we've been spending, uh, so much time together and, you know…" Was Toby nervous? His voice tripped over the words like a shy schoolboy asking her out to prom. He was usually so confident. What had happened to all his swagger and self-assuredness?

"So they want to check me out?" She actually wanted to ask if they were trying to determine if she was good enough for their Fortune Jones standards. Angie had the feeling she wouldn't pass that test.

"It's really not a big deal. It's just a little family get-together. And I made Stacey promise that they wouldn't interrogate you or anything."

"Yeah, that's not exactly selling me on the idea, Toby." In fact, the implication that he probably had to wrestle the promise from his sister made it seem that much more likely that what his family had planned was a full-scale inquisition.

"Well, I figure we could either go to the dinner together and show a kind of united front, or we can sit back and wait for them to come into the Superette one by one and hound you for information."

That was a good point. She didn't relish being the subject of the Fortune Joneses' scrutiny, but she'd rather it be in the privacy of their family ranch than in public at her place of employment. She didn't mind working in the bakery on occasion, but she'd hate to have to hide back there for good.

"Plus," Toby continued, "the kids will be there and Stacey is bringing Piper. If we stick close to at least one of the children, we should be safe, right?"

Angie didn't know if he meant they'd be safe from the prying questions from his family or safe from their own raging hormones.

But she just wasn't sure she should go. She wanted to spend more time with him, but would this just make things more complicated? He sounded as if he was eager to have her there, which wasn't how a man would act if he was trying to break it off with a woman.

"Let me think about it," she finally said.

"Fair enough. I'll be at the baseball field most of the afternoon, so just give me a call on my cell when you decide."

She had no more than set her phone down on the counter when a preprogrammed ringtone sounded. The foreboding theme song from *Jaws* indicated it was her mother.

Doris had called her twice last night, and if Angie didn't talk to her mom now, the woman would think something was going on and make another surveillance trip into the Superette.

"Hi, Mom," Angie finally said, ending the crescendo of doom.

"Evangeline, I've been trying to get ahold of you since yesterday. Where have you been? On a date?"

Did her mom suspect?

Probably not. Doris didn't keep in touch with many people she'd known from when she'd lived in Horseback Hollow. They were too small-town for Doris's perceived cosmopolitan lifestyle. Not that Lubbock could be considered an epicenter of sophistication by most people's standards, but her mom liked to think she was a big deal now.

"I've just been really busy. Nothing new or exciting going on here."

"Good, because if you don't have plans tonight, there's a dinner dance at the country club here in Lubbock, and Margie Suttelheimer's grandson is going to be there. He's a corporate attorney, and his second divorce was just finalized last month. Margie assured me his prenup was ironclad. His ex barely got a dime, so he's still worth millions."

Angie had never made a quicker decision.

"I'm sorry, Mom. I've already made plans for tonight."

She'd just have to tell Toby that dinner with the Fortune Jones clan was on.

At one minute after nine, Toby went out to the barn for some privacy. Using his cell phone, he placed a call to Ms. Fisk at child services, only to reach a recording that said she was out of the office. So he left her a voice-mail message.

Next he called the Lubbock attorney who'd first contacted him about the money that the anonymous donor had given him and he'd placed in trust for the kids. Jake Gleason specialized in estate planning, so if push came to shove, Toby would retain someone else to handle the custody issue. But for right now, he needed some professional assurance that Barbara had only been blowing smoke.

Unfortunately, Jake hadn't been able to do much to ease his worry. "It's hard to second-guess what the court will decide in cases like yours. One judge may consider stability a priority and look at how well the kids are doing under your care and not want to move them. But another might prefer to keep kids with their family members."

Jake did, however, give Toby the names of a couple of family-law attorneys.

As morning wore on, the only thing that had given

Toby a lift had been thoughts of Angie. Her bright-eyed smile and upbeat nature had a way of making him feel as though everything would work out fine—one way or another. So he hoped she still planned to join them at his parents' house.

By the time lunch was over and afternoon rolled around, he'd picked up the phone a couple of times to call her, just to make sure they were still on for dinner. After all, she'd been known to change her mind.

Finally, at three o'clock, he bit the bullet and called. When she answered, he asked, "Are we still on for that barbecue at my parents' house?"

"Sure. What time did you want to go?"

"I thought I'd pick you up around four."

"You shouldn't have to drive all the way into town to get me when your parents live closer to you. Why don't I drive to your place? Then I can fix Kylie's hair."

"That makes more sense. And Kylie would really appreciate a woman's hand with those pigtails. I can never seem to get them to hang evenly."

Angie laughed, and the lilt of her voice made him grip the phone tighter, as if he could draw her near and hold her close.

"While I was helping Mr. Murdock organize his closets, I found some ribbons in an old sewing basket. He said I could have them, so I'll bring them with me. I also baked brownies to take with us. I'm ready now, so I may as well head on over to your place."

"That sounds like a plan. I'll round up the troops, and we'll be ready when you get here."

"By the way," Angie said, "who's going to be at that family dinner?"

"My parents, of course. My sister Delaney and my

brother Galen. Stacey is the ringleader, so she and her fiancé, Colton Foster, will be there, along with her baby, Piper. I imagine my brother Jude and his fiancée, Gabriella Mendoza, will be coming. And of course Liam and Julia Tierney."

"It'll be fun to see Julia outside of the Superette," Angie said. "And it will be nice to see Stacey and Delaney again."

Toby hoped she still felt that way after his sisters began plying her with questions about their supposed relationship.

"It might be best not to mention my brother Chris," Toby said. "Unless someone else brings him up first."

"Why?"

He waited a beat, wondering why he felt inclined to even mention it.

"It's not as though there's a big family rift," he explained, trying to downplay things and to choose his words carefully. "It's just there were some hard feelings about him leaving Horseback Hollow and moving to Red Rock."

"That's really not a secret. There's been some talk around town. And Sawyer and Laurel made a comment about it at the flight school."

"What did they say?" Toby asked.

"Nothing really. They don't discuss things like that in front of their employees. But they said something in passing, and I connected a few dots. So I know that Chris is working for Sawyer's dad at the Fortune Foundation. But that's about it."

Toby didn't know much more than that, either, although he'd been tempted to go to Red Rock and talk to his brother face-to-face. But with him now having three kids, all of whom were in school and involved in outside activities, he wasn't free to make a trip like that without a lot of juggling and some careful orchestrating.

"I'm assuming that your parents aren't happy about his move," Angie said.

Toby didn't usually air family laundry in public, but he and Angie had become pretty close lately, so sharing his concerns came easily. "When my mom asked us to accept our roots by taking on the Fortune name, my dad was a good sport about it. But when Chris announced he was moving to Red Rock, my dad hit the roof. He felt as though my brother had completely jumped ship by leaving town and going to work for James Marshall Fortune. Things really hit the fan then."

There'd always been issues between Chris and their dad over the years, although Toby never had thought they were all that serious. But apparently, he'd been wrong.

"Don't worry about me saying anything at dinner tonight—or to anyone else," Angie said. "I may have my faults, but being a gossip isn't one of them."

"Thanks. I appreciate that."

Silence filled the line for a beat, then Angie said, "I'd better let you go. I'll see you in a little while."

As soon as they ended the call, Toby rounded up the kids and told them to wash up, change their clothes and get ready to go to Grandma and Grandpa's house.

They might not be related by blood, but his parents and siblings had accepted them into the Fortune Jones

fold, just as though they were. And the kids, who'd
been starved for love and affection, had been thrilled
to have a family to call their own. So the last time
they'd visited, his mom had suggested they not be so
formal. "Why don't y'all call us Grandma Jeanne and
Grandpa Deke?" she'd said.

The kids, who'd never really had parents, let alone
grandparents, had jumped at the chance to become
a part of Jeanne's brood. In fact, if you didn't know,
you'd think there'd been a long line of redheads somewhere in the Fortune Jones family tree.

Toby did, however, realize that it could all come to
an end one day if Barbara made good on her threat,
and his gut twisted at the possibility. But he shook off
the negative thoughts and tried to focus on the fact that
the kids were thriving. And that their school would
back that up if need be.

"Can I pack my backpack with things me and Piper
can play with?" Kylie asked.

Toby smiled. Most little girls loved dolls, but having a real baby to play with? "Absolutely. Just let Aunt
Stacey check out the toys first. You know how careful she is about the things Piper puts in her mouth."

"I will," Kylie said, as she dashed off to her room.

Toby glanced at the clock on the mantel. While the
kids were getting ready, he'd take a shower. Angie
would be here before he knew it.

Chapter Eight

Nearly an hour later, Angie arrived at the Double H wearing a white sundress that was wholesome, yet strappy and sexy at the same time—especially when paired with brown cowboy boots.

"Look what I have," she said, lifting a platter of gooey-looking brownies in one hand and a fistful of colorful hair ribbons in the other.

"Nice," Toby said, although he was far more focused on the sweet and lovely lady who stood in front of him, her blue eyes bright, her brown hair lying soft and glossy along her almost bare shoulders.

"Where's Kylie?" she asked.

"In her room. I'll call her." But before Toby could open his mouth, Kylie came dashing into the entry to greet Angie.

The two of them took off, and before long, Kylie

returned, wearing a pair of cowboy boots, just like Angie, her hair in princess-perfect pigtails.

"Let's go," he said.

It took only ten minutes on the county road to reach his parents' ranch. After driving through the white wooden gate, Toby followed the graveled road to the house and parked near the barn, next to the other cars and trucks.

"Looks like everyone beat us here," he said.

"Are we late?" Angie asked.

"Not really. But I have a feeling the women in my family were eager to be here when we arrived."

"Why?"

"Curiosity, I suppose." Toby shut off the ignition. "They know we've been seeing a lot of each other, and I'm afraid their imaginations are getting the best of them."

He could argue—and, in fact, he had argued—that he and Angie weren't dating, that she was merely helping him out with the kids. But sexual attraction and mutual interest were definitely flaring beneath the surface, and he wasn't so sure he'd be able to keep that a secret, especially here.

They all got out of the truck. As usual, the kids managed to pile out a lot faster than they ever climbed in.

"Don't forget to wipe your feet at the front door," Toby called out to them. "And don't barge in. Hang on until Angie and I get there."

"We won't," they called back in near unison.

Toby waited for Angie, as she reached into the cab and pulled out a denim jacket. Then she slipped into it, covering the white sundress that revealed a lovely set of tanned arms and shoulders. But as afternoon wore into evening, he knew there was a chance it could get chilly, so he couldn't blame her for being prepared.

Next he watched as she reached into the cab for the platter of brownies she'd brought.

"I'm sorry," she said, as she realized he was standing near the truck, waiting for her. "I didn't mean to be a slug."

"No problem." He actually liked watching her. But if he stared at her any longer, thinking about how much he wanted to pull her close, to kiss her before entering the house, it was going to take a whole lot more than an evening breeze to cool him off.

They walked together, meeting up with the kids at the front door, which was flanked by large pots of colorful flowers.

Out of habit, Toby took care to wipe his boots, just as he'd asked the children to do.

"My mom always made a big deal about us coming inside with muddy feet." He chuckled as he reached for the doorknob to let them all into the house. "I guess some habits are hard to break."

Toby's mom, with her silver hair pulled into a bun and dressed in her usual stretch-denim jeans and a pale blue sweatshirt, greeted them in the foyer. She gave Toby a warm embrace, then took the time to address each of the kids.

"Now, don't you look pretty, Kylie. Look at those yellow ribbons in your hair. And my goodness. What in the world have you stuffed in that backpack?"

"Toys to show baby Piper. Is she here?"

Jeanne Marie placed a hand on Kylie's head and smiled. "She certainly is. Aunt Stacey just gave her some bananas and peaches for a snack, which she's washing off her face and hands now. Why don't you go into the kitchen and see if she's ready to play."

"Oh, good," Kylie said, as she dashed off.

"And you boys are in for a big treat," Jeanne Marie told Brian and Justin. "Grandpa Deke fixed the rungs to the tree house and gave it a new coat of paint yesterday. And when Uncle Galen saw what he'd done, he attached a rope swing to one of those sturdy ole branches. You probably ought to go check it out."

"Cool," Brian said, as both boys hurried off.

Well done, Toby thought. His mother adored the kids, but it was plain to see that she had something up her sleeve. She'd sent them off happily so she could devote her full attention to Angie and to the interrogation process.

Now, with the children out of the way, she welcomed Angie with a warm shake of the hand. "I'm so glad you could join us. Toby tells me how helpful you've been to him this past week."

"It's been my pleasure. The kids are great. And in all honesty, Toby's so good with them, I'm not sure he even needs my help at all."

"Don't let her downplay her efforts," Toby said. "She's been awesome, whether it's playing beauty salon with Kylie or planning a make-it-yourself pizza night or watching a movie under the stars. And I would have really been up a creek yesterday without her."

"You don't say." His mom smiled, those blue eyes glimmering. "I'll tell you what, Toby. Why don't you check out that tree house and make sure Galen secured that swing right, while I take Angie into the kitchen. Since she's such a good helper, I'm going to rope her into helping the girls and I finish up with the burger fixings."

And just like a mama fox, Jeanne Marie had dispensed with Toby.

He could argue and insist that Angie stick close to his side, he supposed. But Angie was a big girl and had proved that she could hold her own. Besides, he wanted to check out that old fort he and his brothers used to play in. And on top of that, he trusted his mom and his sisters not to go overboard.

So he took his leave, walking out to the backyard, where his own interrogation undoubtedly awaited.

Angie followed Toby's mother out to the kitchen. She'd always liked the woman, but then, who in town didn't?

Jeanne Marie might come across as plain and simple, but there was more to her than met the eye. She had a quick wit, a gentle spirit and a kind heart. She also loved her husband and children dearly and was fiercely devoted to them.

Since working at the Superette, Angie had picked up on all of that. She'd even found herself a bit envious of the family's closeness. How could she not be?

She'd always wanted to be part of a big, happy family, but she'd been an only child. She and her daddy had been close, but he'd died five years ago.

Now that Angie was an adult, her mom sought the closeness they'd never quite had before. But Doris

Edwards was so determined to make Angie into the woman she wanted her to be that it was easier to avoid her, which was sad.

"I brought some brownies," Angie said, holding out the platter of chocolaty squares covered in caramel frosting and toffee pieces.

"You didn't need to do that," Jeanne Marie said, as she led Angie through the large-but-cozy living room. "But it was awfully nice of you. I try to have plenty for everyone to eat, but I have to admit, this family can really put away the desserts. So I doubt you'll have anything to take home except a few crumbs."

When they reached the kitchen, Angie saw Piper sitting in a walker on the floor with Kylie playing beside her. The little red-haired girl had made fast work of emptying out the entire contents of her backpack on the hardwood floor.

"You girls remember Angie," Jeanne Marie said to both Stacey and Delaney.

"Of course." Stacey, a bright-eyed blonde with a light spray of freckles on her nose, smiled. "We're so glad Toby finally brought you out to meet his crazy family."

Angie and Stacey had graduated from high school together, although they really hadn't run in the same circles. Stacey, who'd gone on to nursing school after graduation, had been more of an academic and tended to hang out with the smarter kids. And Angie had been all over the campus, hanging with the members of whichever social club she was trying out that semester.

"Thanks for including me." Angie placed the brownies on the sideboard, next to a Bundt cake in a covered dish and a plate of lemon bars. Toby's mom had been right. They were certainly dessert-friendly in this household. She hoped everyone was as sweet as the offerings on the countertop.

"Can I help you guys with anything?" Angie asked, noticing that Stacey was putting the finishing touches on a cheese-and-vegetable platter.

"Julia and Gabi are setting the tables outside," Delaney said, as she stirred something that appeared to be potato salad. "And we're almost done in here."

"Why don't you pull up a chair?" Stacey nodded to one of the empty barstools on the other side of the kitchen island. "Tell us what you've been doing with yourself since high school."

"Now hold off a moment," Jeanne Marie said. "It's only fair to offer Angie a glass of wine or some iced tea first. The least we can do is let our guest wet her whistle before you launch into a full-blown question-and-answer session."

When Jeanne winked at Angie, and her daughters laughed, easing the awkward tension, Angie couldn't help but join in the merriment. If Stacey and Delaney could make light of their overly curious natures, then so could she. Besides, she had nothing to hide.

Well, nothing except the fact that she had the hots for one of their brothers.

"I think I'll take an iced tea," Angie said, "but you guys keep doing what you're doing. I'll get it."

She'd no more than crossed the kitchen and was reaching for the pitcher when Justin rushed into the room, his eyes bright, his excitement impossible to ignore. "Angie, I was telling Uncle Galen about your candy brownies, and he wanted me to bring them out to the tree house so we can all try them."

If there was anyone who loved sweets more than the Fortune Jones family, it was Justin Hemings. And since he'd been eyeing those brownies and asking for a taste ever since she'd arrived at the Double H, Angie knew when he was still trying to finagle an early treat.

"You tell Uncle Galen that we have so many desserts to choose from that it's best if he waits until after dinner. That way, instead of having only one treat, he'll be able to try them all." Angie pointed to the counter holding the sweets.

Justin hurried over to look at his many options. His eyes darted from side to side, unable to settle on a favorite.

"Did you make all of these?" he asked Angie. Before she could answer, he looked at Jeanne Marie and continued. "Angie makes the *best* cupcakes with little race cars on the top. And she makes us pizza with our very own favorite toppings. And she puts extra butter on the popcorn because that's how Toby likes it best. She's the best cooker in the world. I'm going to tell Brian about the desserts. C'mon, Angie. You gotta come see the tree house."

And with that, Justin shot out the open sliding door, running as fast as he talked.

Angie looked at Toby's sisters, who both seemed eager to pounce on her with questions, but Jeanne Marie saved her by saying, "Let's go see the tree house. Then you can meet my husband. That will give my daughters plenty of time to strategize about what they want to ask you."

Grateful to have escaped what she was sure would have been a barrage of questions, Angie tossed them each a smile and went outside with Jeanne Marie to a built-in barbecue, where Deke was preparing to grill hamburger patties and hot dogs.

"Honey," Jeanne Marie said, "this is Angie Edwards, Toby's friend."

Deke, a tall, rugged man with a thatch of thick gray hair, turned to Angie and greeted her with a hint of a smile. "It's nice to meet you. We like it when the kids bring their friends home."

"I'm glad to be included," Angie said. "Where's that tree house I heard so much about?"

Deke pointed about fifty yards from the house to a huge tree where Toby stood with his brothers Jude, Liam and Galen. The men were watching Brian swing while laughing at something Liam said.

"The boys found that ole fort the first day Toby brought them to the ranch," Deke said. "But we hadn't realized how rotten some of that lumber had gotten until Justin fell and bumped his head a couple of weeks ago. So we wouldn't let them play on it until I could find the time to replace some of those old boards."

"Well, it looks as though they appreciate your time and effort," Angie said. "In fact, if I wasn't wearing a dress, I'd join them on that swing."

Jeanne Marie laughed. "And I might take a turn with you. When our sons were little, we used to have overnight campouts in that fort."

"You slept outside with them?" Angie couldn't imagine her mom doing something like that.

"I did until they stopped being afraid of the bogeyman. After that, whenever they had those campouts I stayed inside and enjoyed the peace and quiet with their daddy."

Deke grinned and gave Jeanne Marie a little pat.

It was heartwarming to see such a loving couple. She'd never seen her parents show each other any affection.

"Honey," Deke said to his wife, "can you please go in the house and get a clean platter for me to put the cooked meat on?"

"I'll get it," Angie offered. "Everyone else has a job to do. I better earn my dinner, too."

"Then you go on ahead," Jeanne Marie said with a laugh. "We wouldn't want you to feel excluded."

Angie started toward the house, just as Julia Tierney was coming outside with a pitcher of lemonade and a stack of red plastic cups.

"Hey," Julia said. "I heard you were coming. It's nice to see you outside of the Superette."

Angie smiled. "It's nice to be here. In fact, I've only been on the ranch a few minutes, but everyone has been so warm and welcoming. You're lucky to be a part of this."

Julia, who'd recently become engaged to Toby's brother Liam, had a glow about her these days. "I've really been blessed. I've fallen in love with the greatest guy in the world, and he has a wonderful family."

"You know," Angie said, as she stepped aside, "I'd better let you put that lemonade down before you drop it. Besides, I finally have a job to do and don't want Deke to think I'm lagging."

Julia smiled. "I'll talk to you later."

As Julia passed through the doorway and onto the patio, Gabriella Mendoza followed behind her, carrying a platter of lettuce leaves, tomato slices and other hamburger fixings.

Gabi was also sporting a diamond engagement ring these days, courtesy of Jude, another of Toby's brothers. The two had met after Gabi's father, Orlando Mendoza, had been seriously injured in a plane crash.

Orlando had been a pilot for the Redmond Flight School when the accident happened. And Gabi had flown out from Miami to be with him as soon as she'd gotten the news.

"Hi there," Gabi said. "It's good to see you again."

"Same here," Angie said. "How's your dad doing?"

"Much better. Thank you for asking."

"I'm so glad to hear that." Angie again stepped aside to let Gabi pass, then entered the kitchen, which was a bustle of activity as Stacey and Delaney laid out plates of appetizers to go outside.

"Your dad asked me to bring him a clean platter for the cooked meat," Angie said.

"I'll get that for you." Stacey went to a side cupboard and pulled out a large, ceramic platter. "But before you go, I do have a question for you."

Angie smiled. "Okay, shoot."

"In high school you were Queen of the First Date and president of just about every club they offered." Angie assumed Stacey was going to point out the obvious—that Angie couldn't commit to anything—until she added, "At times I was a bit envious."

No kidding? She hadn't meant to insult her? Stacey had actually admired her?

"I'm curious," Stacey said. "When you told Justin not to choose anything too soon, how did you come up with that strategy?"

It was a strategy, although no one had actually pegged it as such.

The other women in the kitchen—Julia and Gabi were now back—continued to move about, but their movements slowed and their side conversations stalled.

Angie had never tried to explain it to anyone before, but for some reason, she opted for candor now. "My dad used to tell me to be careful when making a choice, because once I made it, I couldn't change my mind. So I took that to heart. I try everything once, knowing that when I find something I'm passionate about, I'll stick to it."

Trouble was, she wasn't entirely convinced of that. If it turned out she was wrong, she could end up in some eternal revolving door of new beginnings and never find a happy ending.

"But you don't believe that, do you?" Delaney said. "I mean, everyone makes mistakes. It's not like you can't start over and have a second chance."

Angie had never talked about her childhood to anyone before, but being here with Toby's family had a way of making her lower her guard.

"Yes, I know that—intellectually. However, I grew up in a household with parents who remained in an unhappy marriage for my sake. And they drilled it into me that once a commitment was made, you had to stick to it."

"That's kind of sad," Delaney said.

"I know. My mom hated small-town life, so living

in Horseback Hollow nearly sucked the life out of her. And as a result, her unhappiness nearly sucked the life out of my dad."

"Is that why your mom eventually moved to Lubbock?" Delaney asked.

It was common knowledge that Doris acted as though she was better than everyone in town. And that she'd filed for a divorce and moved to Lubbock the day after Angie had graduated from high school.

Still, even when her mom had lived with them in Horseback Hollow, she'd commuted to work in Lubbock, which meant she was gone most of the time. And to be honest, she'd left Angie and her father emotionally even before that—or so it had seemed.

"My parents were mismatched from day one," Angie said. "And, if anything, it's made me not want to make any big decisions that I might regret for the rest of my life, especially when it came to a college degree or a lifelong profession."

"C'mon, Angie," Delaney said. "Don't you think you're taking your dad's advice to an extreme?"

"Maybe," Angie conceded. "But I've had a lot of cool jobs, tried a variety of things and learned a lot along the way. I can also handle just about anything thrown my way."

"I've heard about some of your job experience," Jeanne Marie said, as she entered the kitchen and breezed right into the conversation.

"What have you heard?" Angie asked.

"That you're more than qualified to do *my* job." Jeanne Marie laughed as she carried the big bowl of potato salad out the back door to the tables set up in the yard.

Angie looked at Toby's sisters and whispered, "What's your mom's job?"

The girls both laughed, and Angie began to wonder whether any of them would answer. Finally, Delaney said, "She was a professional stay-at-home mom."

Angie was at a loss. She could never be a stay-at-home mom. Not like Jeanne Marie.

When the girls finally got their giggles under control, Stacey asked, "Do you need any help deciding what to do with our brother?"

"No, not really. We never seem to have any time to talk about it. So I have no idea what he's even thinking."

Angie did, however, have a very memorable moment of waking in his arms—before the sprinklers ruined it all.

"You mean you've never had a proper date?" Stacey asked.

"I'm afraid not. The kids are always with us. And to tell you the truth, I don't know if Toby *wants* to date me."

"Oh, believe us," Stacey said, "he wants to."

Delaney beamed. "Just leave it to us. Stacey and I are just the ones who can make that happen."

A date? With Toby Fortune Jones?

Angie didn't know if she should run for the hills— or thank her lucky stars.

As the meat sizzled on the grill, setting off the aroma of barbecued burgers and hot dogs, Toby stood next to his father and Colton Foster, Stacey's fiancé.

Deke had roped his future son-in-law into helping

him man the grill, and the two ranchers had been discussing the rising cost of feed corn, as well as the new bull Deke intended to purchase.

But Toby couldn't seem to focus on the discussion at hand. Instead he kept thinking about the one going on in the kitchen, where the women had gathered with Angie.

"Excuse me," he said, as he stepped away from his dad and Colton.

The two men continued to talk while Toby strode across the patio to the insulated cooler that held a variety of drinks, including the ice-cold bottle of beer he snatched for himself.

So far, the family dinner at his parents' house seemed to be going well. The women had begun to carry out the food and place it on tables that had been set up on the lawn, which meant it would be time to eat soon.

Jude, Liam and Galen had gathered near the tree house, where they were probably still reminiscing about their childhood or predicting the likelihood of the Rangers making it to the World Series this year.

But Toby's mind was on the kids and the fear that he might lose them. He could honestly say that if Barbara were a loving and maternal woman who'd made a few mistakes and was trying hard to straighten her life out he wouldn't be so uneasy. After all, he probably valued family ties more than anyone. It was just that he'd never seen a maternal side to Barbara.

He thought about sharing his worries with his family, but he didn't want to talk about it in front of the kids. Maybe it was best to wait until after he'd talked to Ms. Fisk on Monday—assuming she'd return his call the day she returned to the office.

Either way, he couldn't very well stew about it all weekend. So he'd better shake it off for now and start mingling before people started asking him what was bothering him.

As he stood in the center of the yard, a beer in hand, debating which of the two male groups to join, a squeal of feminine laughter rang out from the kitchen.

What in the heck were the women talking about in there? He hoped the topic of conversation wasn't on him and Angie.

Should he check? Did Angie need him to bail her out?

No, they were all laughing, so it had to be something else. His presence would only remind them of the questioning they'd planned upon his and Angie's arrival. So it would be best—and safer—if he hung out with the men.

Opting for the rowdier group near the tree house, Toby returned to the cooler, reached in for a couple more Coronas and carried them out to his brothers.

Upon his approach, a big ole grin stole across Galen's face. "You're just the guy I wanted to talk to."

"What about?" Toby asked.

"About you and Angie. I hear things are heating up."

Toby wasn't sure where Galen had come up with that. He glanced at Jude and Liam, both of whom were smirking, and realized it was now his turn to get the third degree. But there wasn't much to tell—or much he was willing to talk about.

He offered up the extra two Coronas he held instead. "You guys want a beer?"

Liam and Jude both took one.

Galen crossed his arms, his grin bursting into a full-on smile. "Don't change the subject, little bro. We just want to know what's going on with you and Angie, especially since Justin told us you two had a sleepover last night."

Aw, hell. Toby had been afraid that was going to happen.

He blew out a sigh. "As nice as that might sound, I'm afraid Justin blew that all out of proportion. Angie stayed over, but it's not what you're thinking."

"Hmm." Liam crossed his arms. "So if it would have been nice, does that mean you're interested in her?"

So what if he was?

Still, Toby wasn't going to admit anything. If he did, he'd never hear the end of it. And besides, he and Angie hadn't even talked about whether they wanted their relationship or friendship or whatever the hell it was to progress to a level like that.

"You know what I think?" Toby said to Liam. "You guys have fallen in love, so you think everyone else ought to be feeling the same way."

"I'm still single and unattached," Galen said. "And I think there's definitely some big-time sparks going on between you and Angie."

"Okay," Toby said. "I'm attracted to her. She's fun to be with. But that's about all there is to it."

"Why aren't you pursuing anything more?" Galen asked.

All kinds of reasons. The kids, for one. Angie's inability to commit to anyone or anything, for another. But then again, that hadn't seemed to matter when they'd woken up in each other's arms this morning.

Of course, there was also the matter of Jude dating her in the past. And Toby didn't want to cross any weird fraternal boundaries or become romantically involved with a woman his brother had once been… intimate with.

Wouldn't that be one huge disappointment?

"Speaking of Angie," Toby said to Jude, "you dated her, didn't you?"

"I guess you could call it that. We only went out a couple of times. It ended pretty abruptly."

"What happened?" Toby asked.

"When Angie's mom saw her out with me one evening, she flipped out. Apparently, she thought Angie could do a whole lot better. Doris tried to lower her voice, but I overheard her refer to me as a 'Horseback Hollow Casanova' and ask if I'd gone through all the women in my own age bracket and had started on a new generation." Jude blew out a sigh. "Okay, granted, there was a six-year age difference, but come on. A whole generation?"

Knowing her mom, that didn't surprise Toby. So if he and Angie ever did start dating, he and Doris would have to set some definite boundaries.

"So it ended quickly," Toby said. "But how serious were you?"

"It never would have gotten off the ground. She was a little too indecisive for me." Jude laughed. "Don't get me wrong. She's a nice girl, and we had fun. But

I made the mistake of asking her which movie she wanted to see. If I hadn't picked one myself and taken her by the hand, we probably would have stood outside the theater all night."

Toby had never really seen that side of Angie. She always seemed to know just what she wanted when she was with him and the kids.

Feminine voices grew louder as the women gathered outside and his mother announced that it was time to eat.

"Brian and Justin," she called to the boys in the tree house, "go on in the house with Kylie and wash your hands."

As the boys hurried to do as they were told, Jude asked Toby, "Has Angie decided upon a career yet?"

"No, she hasn't."

"Don't let that stop you," Galen said. "Look at her. She's smoking hot."

His oldest brother certainly had that right. Toby studied the lovely brunette crossing the lawn in that white sundress. She had on the denim jacket now, as well as those cowboy boots. So she'd covered up her arms and shoulders. But she still looked good.

In fact, she looked amazing in whatever she wore—especially a wet yoga outfit.

"Let me know if you're not interested in her," Galen added. "If that's the case, I might ask her out myself."

Just the thought of Galen moving in on Angie sent Toby's senses reeling.

"All right, I'm interested," he admitted. "So back off."

Before his brothers could tease him further, he

headed for the tables and found seats for him, Angie and the kids.

As was typical of a Fortune Jones dinner, everyone ate their fill, including the variety of desserts. All the while, they told stories about growing up together, sometimes teasing, usually smiling or laughing.

When Toby could finally call it a day, he rounded up the kids and told them it was time to head home.

"Why don't you let Brian and Justin spend the night here," Galen said. "I think I'll camp out in that tree house for old times' sake. And it would be nice if the boys kept me company."

Before Toby could respond, Stacey chimed in. "And Piper would like to have her very first sleepover. Why don't you let Colton and me take Kylie home with us?"

"A sleepover?" Toby asked. "Piper is only nine months old."

Stacey smiled. "You're right. She doesn't stay up past seven. But then I'll get a chance to play with Kylie."

What was going on? Galen and Stacey were offering to keep the kids?

"I don't know about that," Toby said. "They don't have their pajamas or toothbrushes."

Galen elbowed him. "Come on, Toby. Real cowboys don't sleep in jammies. They sleep in their boots and clothes. What's the matter with you?"

Stacey edged forward. "Kylie can sleep in one of my old T-shirts. I also have a brand-new toothbrush she can use. What do you say?"

He didn't know what to say. The offer stole the words right out of him.

"Come on, Toby." His little sister gave him a wink. "You deserve a good night's sleep."

It took him a moment to realize what his crazy family was up to. And he didn't know if he should kill them or kiss them. But when he took a look at Angie, when he spotted the wide-eyed wonder, the look of surprise...

Well, it wasn't just the kids who were whooping it up and begging for the night to come.

Toby's hormones were right there with them.

Chapter Nine

As Toby's pickup headed down the county road that led to the Double H Ranch, Angie bit down on her bottom lip and stared out the windshield. It was the first time they'd actually been alone, and for some reason they both seemed to be at a loss for words.

Sure, they'd had a few stolen moments before, but this was different. There were no children to worry about walking in on them, no job to hustle out to, no errands to run.

It was just the two of them.

The silence in the cab was almost overwhelming, and if that weren't enough, Angie's heart was zipping through her chest, racing around as if it wanted to beat her and Toby back to his place.

But then what? Things were sure to be more awkward there.

Would he tell her good-night the minute they got out of the truck? Or would he invite her into the house?

He hadn't uttered a word since they'd left, so she had no idea what he was thinking. But whenever she stole a glance across the seat, the expression he wore suggested that he felt just as on edge and nervous as she did.

She'd like to put him—or rather both of them—at ease, but she was so far out of her element that she didn't know where to begin.

What she could really use was an icebreaker, but she couldn't seem to come up with anything clever to say or do. So she just sank into the leather passenger seat, trying to keep her eyes off the handsome rancher who'd been captivating her thoughts more and more each day.

When they finally turned down his drive and neared the ranch house, she spotted her car parked right where she'd left it. The old Toyota looked a little sad and lonely sitting there, and Angie was going to feel the same way if she drove off in it.

Think, girl. Say something.

"So," she finally said, the sound of her voice breaking into the silence. "What are you going to do with an evening all to yourself?"

At that, Toby turned, glanced across the seat at her and smiled. "It's been so long since I've had a night without the kids that I have no idea."

Angie tucked a strand of hair behind her ear and tossed him a carefree grin. "Then if I were you, I'd turn on the TV, choose a channel that doesn't play cartoons and eat ice cream straight from the container."

Toby shut off the ignition. In the dim light of the

cab, she caught a glimmer in his eyes and a flirtatious tilt in his smile.

Now there went a definite *zing*.

He stretched his arm across the seat, and his smile deepened. "If you were me, would you invite someone in to watch television and help you eat the rest of the chocolate ice cream?"

"Actually, that's exactly what I'd do. But instead of the ice cream, I'd offer her wine because she probably avoided anything alcoholic at the barbecue for fear she'd slip and say something that your sisters might misconstrue. But I'd also promise to let her control the remote."

Toby laughed. "The wine, I can do. But I'm pretty territorial about my remote."

Not bad for an icebreaker, huh?

Angie smiled, then reached for the door handle and let herself out of the truck. They walked together to the porch, and when Toby opened the front door for her and flipped on the light switch, she stepped inside.

The house was quieter than it had ever been, at least since she'd started coming to visit. Only now, the solitude made things awkward again. Without the kids around to act as buffers, she and Toby had to face each other and whatever they were feeling.

He led her to the kitchen, where he opened the fridge and pulled out the bottle of wine for her and a longneck beer for him.

"I had a lot of fun tonight," she said, as she removed a goblet from the cabinet. "Your family knows how to have a good time. And they're down-to-earth."

"If by 'down-to-earth,' you mean 'meddling,' then,

yes. They are." Toby filled her glass. After popping the top off his drink, he leaned against the counter in a sexy cowboy slant.

"They weren't meddling," Angie said. "They were a little curious, maybe. But friendly. And look at how helpful they were, offering to take the kids for the night so that you could have a break."

Toby chuckled, then lifted the Corona to his lips and took another swig.

Oh, sweet goodness. Those lips. Angie had never been so jealous of a drink container.

When he lowered the bottle, his gaze zeroed in on her. "You know why they offered to keep the kids, don't you?"

She hadn't wanted to speculate, but now that he'd brought it up, she supposed, deep down, that she'd known what they'd been up to. They'd wanted to give her and Toby some time alone.

Or rather, a *night* alone.

Gosh. It was sure getting warm in here. Had someone left the oven on while they'd been gone?

She slipped off her denim jacket and placed it on the back of one of the barstools. All the while, Toby continued to lean against the counter, watching her.

Why was he looking at her like that—as if there was a big ole elephant in the room and he was determined to circle around it and come right on over to her?

His gaze was only making her warmer, and if he didn't stop, she was going to melt into a puddle.

Hoping the wine would help her cool down, she took a gulp.

"Come on." Toby reached for her hand, his fingers

threading through hers and sending a flurry of little zings rushing all the way to her core. Then he led her to the living room.

Thank goodness they were walking. Her knees had turned to rubber, and she wasn't sure they'd hold her up much longer if she didn't shake them out and get the blood flowing again.

She could use some cool air, too.

When they reached the living room, he led her to the leather sectional, where she took a seat. Then he sat next to her, even though there'd been plenty of room to spread out.

That was a good sign, yes?

Or was it a bad one?

She wasn't quite sure. But either way, the heat from the kitchen had followed them into the living room, and she took another swallow of wine.

"My family was definitely meddling," he said. "They could have kept the kids last night—or the weekend before. But they wanted to spend some time with you first, to see us together, before they made the offer."

"So they were vetting me?" she asked.

"That's about the size of it."

"Hmm." Angie stared at her chardonnay as if it was the most fascinating wine she'd ever tasted. Then she took another sip. If she continued to drink at this rate, she'd finish what was left in the bottle—and be on the floor soon after that.

"I guess I should be flattered that they approve," she said.

He placed his arm along the backrest, close enough

for her to feel his body heat along her bare shoulders. "How could they not approve of you? You're bright, funny, sweet and genuine." He paused, then fingered a strand of her hair. "And you're so damn beautiful."

Zing! Zing! Zing!

Now her glass was empty. Where had all that cold wine gone?

"Aw, hell," he said. "I'd wanted to spend some time with you away from the kids. But now that I've finally got you alone..."

When he trailed off, she studied his averted gaze, his pained expression.

What had he been about to say?

That he wasn't interested in her? That she was nice as far as babysitters went, but there was no point in her being here if the kids weren't?

"But *now* what?" she prodded.

Whoa. Where had the double-shot of courage come from? Did she really want to hear what he'd been about to say?

Her heart went haywire while she awaited his answer.

Toby removed his hand from her hair, from the back of the sofa and leaned forward.

Uh-oh. Bad sign?

Then he raked his fingers through his own hair. "It's just that now it all feels forced. And expected. It's like every member of my family knows exactly what we're doing right this second."

Angie chuckled, the sound coming out in a nervous rush. "But we aren't doing *anything*. And even if we do decide to do something, whatever happens or doesn't happen is our secret. Nobody has to know."

Toby's brows furrowed, and a look of annoyance crossed his face. "Of course no one will know. Do I look like the type to kiss and tell?"

"Toby," Angie said, her tone the same one she used when one of the kids was out of line. "I'm not sure if you're the type to *kiss,* let alone talk about it."

Their eyes met for a moment, and then a slow grin spread across his face. "Oh, I'm the type, all right." Then he lowered his mouth to hers.

Angie turned into his embrace, eager to kiss him with the passion that had been building over the past week until it threatened to consume her now.

And she wasn't disappointed.

His lips were soft, yet demanding. And his taste, while cool and refreshing, was hot and arousing.

Breaths mingled, tongues mated and the kiss deepened, intensifying until they were making out on the sofa like a couple of teenagers who had the run of the house for the very first time.

As Toby tugged at the strap of her dress, slipping it off her shoulder, he stroked her skin, igniting a fire and an ache deep in her core. Her breath caught, and her zing meter burst, like a flash of sparklers on a Fourth of July night.

As she leaned back and sucked a gulp of air into her lungs, Toby trailed kisses down her neck, along her shoulder. The warmth of his breath, the skill of his lips, caused her back to arch. And she was…his.

Toby had wanted to get Angie into his arms ever since the day he'd seen her wearing those cutoff shorts and walking around with bare, freshly painted toes.

And judging from the wispy little pants and whimpers coming from her sweet lips, she'd been wanting him just as badly.

At least, she certainly wanted him now.

The ride home from his parents' house had just about done him in. He'd never been so tense in his life. Not just because the physical attraction between the two of them had built to astronomical proportions, but because they'd soon have a big decision to make.

If they took things to a physical level tonight, there'd be no going back. And he needed to know that they were both on the same page.

As much as it pained him, he pulled his mouth from hers and ended the kiss.

"I…uh…" He cleared his throat. "We…"

Hell, he didn't even know what to say. Seconds ago, when they'd been kissing, he'd been in complete control of his tongue. But now he could barely form a simple word.

Angie merely looked at him with passion-glazed eyes.

Finally he managed to spell it out. "If you think you might have second thoughts about where this is heading, now would be a good time to say it."

"If you're afraid I'll change my mind or have any regrets," she said, "don't be."

That was the answer he'd wanted to hear. So he captured her mouth in another heart-soaring, star-spinning kiss.

Somehow, without removing her lips from his, she managed to lift a knee, and in one swift movement, she straddled his lap and faced him.

As they continued to kiss, he ran his hands up and down the slope of her back, along her hips, caressing her curves, memorizing them.

The lovely sundress, once so damn sexy, was now in the way. Should he unzip it and do away with it?

As she began to rock back and forth, a movement that was sure to drive them both over the brink, he realized they could very easily make love right on the sofa if he didn't change tactics. So again he drew his lips from hers.

"Let's take this into the bedroom," he whispered. But instead of releasing her, he held her tighter, leaned forward and slowly got to his feet.

She wrapped her legs around his waist, holding on as he carried her to his room. He kissed her along the way, hoping not to step on any of the LEGO pieces or dolls that sometimes littered his hallway.

He meant to hold himself in check, but he couldn't seem to help himself from tumbling with her onto the bed.

As they stretched out, hands reaching, lips seeking, she sobered and pulled away. "Toby, wait."

Oh, no. She wasn't going to stop him now, was she? If so, this was one hell of a time for her to prove everyone right and change her mind.

"I'm not on the pill," she said. "And I don't have any…you know…protection with me. I wasn't really anticipating this."

Did she think *he* was?

He couldn't help but smile, as he rolled to the side, taking her with him. "I hope you don't think I was expecting this to happen, either, or that I planned to bring you back here and ravish you." He'd hoped to, yes. But he hadn't planned to. "I do happen to have some condoms, though."

She smiled. "So we have that hurdle covered."

"And just so you know, I've been weighing the pros and cons of where moving forward might take us."

"Maybe you're overthinking things," she said.

Had that come from the woman who seemed to overthink every little decision she'd ever had to make?

"It's really quite simple," she added. "Either you want me or you don't."

He ran a knuckle along her cheek. "That part *is* simple. I want you more than I've ever wanted another woman in my life."

Dang. Had he really admitted that to her? And was it actually true?

Yeah, he was afraid that it was.

"But then what?" he asked.

"If you're sure about what you want, then everything else will fall into place."

How could he argue with *that* logic?

Toby chuckled and slowly shook his head. Who would have guessed that Angie would be the one helping him make a decision?

But, in truth, he feared he'd decided he wanted her—and wanted this—long before now. And judging by the way she'd sat up, unzipped her dress and began to lift it over her head, so had she.

Toby reached into his nightstand drawer and pulled out the box of condoms he'd picked up at the pharmacy when he'd been in Lubbock yesterday.

Okay, so maybe he *had* done a *little* planning. And

after waking up with her on the lawn this morning in a state of arousal, he'd realized that purchase had been a good investment, since he'd thought—or rather, he'd hoped—an occasion like this might arise.

When Angie had completely undressed, she stretched out on the bed, her perfect breasts, her lush curves a tempting sight he'd never forget.

She was beautiful and sweet and, at least for this moment in time, completely his.

She reached for his belt buckle, letting him know that she was ready for him to join her, and he quickly removed his clothing, too.

"You're so beautiful, Toby. So perfect."

Him? She thought *he* was perfect? She was the beautiful one. The perfect one. And as he lay down beside her again, he used his mouth and his body to tell her just that.

When he entered her, making them one, she arched up to meet his thrusts. And as she peaked, as her nails dug into his shoulders, she called out his name, sending him over the edge of control.

They came together in one amazing kaleidoscope of color, then held on to each other, riding the ebb and flow of the wonder-filled moment to the very end.

Finally, as their breathing slowed to normal, Angie opened her eyes and smiled. "That was amazing."

"To say the least." Toby pressed a kiss on her forehead. "And I have to admit, it was probably one of the best decisions I've ever made."

"Sometimes," Angie said, as she ran a leg along his, "the right decision can't be made with a list and a spreadsheet. Sometimes you just have to follow your heart."

He'd followed his—right into Angie's arms. Trouble was, he feared she'd captured his heart and that he might never get it back, even if she decided she was no longer interested in what little he had to offer her.

After walking naked through the quiet house to the kitchen for the carton of ice cream to share in bed, they made love several times before finally falling to sleep in the wee hours of morning.

The next day, as sunlight peered through the open shutters of his bedroom window, Toby awoke with Angie in his arms, the tousled sheet doing very little to cover her naked body. There was no telling when they'd have the house to themselves again, so he decided to wake her with a kiss.

But before he could nuzzle her neck, the bedside telephone rang, dashing his romantic thoughts.

Angie shot up in bed, pulling the sheet with her, as if the ringing phone had not only awoken her but reminded her their night in paradise had ended.

Toby snatched the telephone receiver after the third ring. "Hello?"

"Hey," Justin said, his voice so loud Angie could undoubtedly hear. "What are you doing? Grandma made us wait until eight o'clock to call you, but we've been up since six."

Bless his mom for putting a time restriction on the morning wake-up call, but would waiting another thirty minutes have hurt?

Angie began to inch off the bed, a pink tint bright-

ening her cheeks. She had a history of running off on
him when they'd been caught in an intimate position,
and Toby wasn't going to let her slip away from him
this time. Not after last night. So he made a grab for
the sheet she was tugging along with her, and she tumbled back to the mattress, practically landing on him.

A muffled "oomph" sounded from her lips, as he
locked his arm around her and pulled her close.

"What was that noise?" Justin asked.

Before Toby could make up a reasonable explanation, Brian yelled, "Don't forget to tell Toby about the
baseball game!"

"Oh, yeah," Justin said. "The reason I called was
because Uncle Galen has tickets for the Lubbock Hub-
bers game today and said he would give them to us. So
can we go? And can we invite Angie? Galen has five
tickets, and the game starts at one. So can we? Please?"

Toby wondered how his brother had magically come
up with exactly five tickets to a minor-league baseball
game the morning after his sisters had concocted a
plan to get him and Angie alone together for the night.
Somehow, it didn't seem like a coincidence.

He put his hand over the mouthpiece and whispered,
"You want to go with us to the ball game?"

Angie's second of hesitation was all he needed to
make the decision for her. After all, she'd been the one
to tell him to follow his heart. So now, in the aftermath of their incredible night together, he was going
to keep following his. And he was going to encourage
her to do the same.

"Okay, kiddo," he told Justin. "I'll call Angie at *her
house* and ask her if she wants to go with us. Then I'll

go by *her house* to get her before I swing by Grandma and Grandpa's house to pick up you guys."

He wondered if he'd gotten his point across that Angie wasn't with him.

But Justin didn't seem to care either way. All he said was "Don't forget to bring our gloves. I'm going to catch the first foul ball!"

"I won't forget."

When they'd said goodbye and the call ended, Toby went back to his very first catch of the day—a beautiful brunette he hoped wouldn't run off on him anytime soon.

Chapter Ten

Toby, Angie and the kids had a blast at the baseball game on Sunday, although Kylie, who'd eaten too much cotton candy, popcorn and too many mustard dogs, had thrown up in Toby's truck on the way home. But both Angie and Toby had gotten used to unpleasant surprises like that—and to rolling with the unexpected punches of life with children.

In fact, it seemed only natural for them to settle into a routine, with Angie spending more time at Toby's than at her own place.

However, Toby was expecting a visit from child services and thought it best to downplay their relationship. Angie, of course, agreed with him, especially since she wasn't sure how involved she wanted to be with him and the kids anyway. So she didn't spend the night with him again. But that didn't mean they weren't able to steal a kiss or enjoy a tender-but-secret embrace whenever they could.

For the next week, they tried to be discreet about the change in their relationship, but their happiness was hard to contain, and the secret began to leak out.

On the following Monday, while the kids were in school, Toby took lunch to her while she was working at Redmond-Fortune Air. She'd stayed so late at the ranch the night before, making out with him on the front porch after the kids went to sleep, that by the time she'd driven home, she'd barely gotten any sleep. And she'd hurried to work without having breakfast.

When Toby had called that morning and learned her alarm hadn't gone off, he'd known she'd be hungry. So he came sauntering in to the flight school carrying a take-out bag from The Grill.

Angie's heart melted at the sight of him, and her stomach growled at the aroma of pastrami and fries.

"What's in the bag?" Sawyer asked his cousin.

"I figured you weren't making enough money to feed your employees," Toby said. "So I brought Angie's lunch."

"Well, it's nice to see you've stopped using the kids as a pretense to schmooze with my most valuable employee."

"I brought one for you, too." Toby tossed one of the wrapped sandwiches to his cousin. "Maybe this will keep your mouth too busy to talk."

Sawyer laughed as he snatched the flying pastrami. "You're going to be buying a lot of extra lunches if you think you can keep the whole town from talking."

Sawyer had been right about that. Angie had heard

a few murmurs while she'd worked at the Superette the next day, although no one came right out and said anything directly to her.

Of course, Mr. Murdock did when she was getting ready to leave for work on Wednesday morning.

"Why don't you take my car," he said, pulling out his set of keys. "Leave yours here, and I'll change the oil for you. When I'm finished, I'll come down to the market and we'll trade."

"That's really sweet of you, Mr. Murdock. Thank you."

"I thought it'd be a shame if you had car trouble and got stranded on the road." He burst into a grin, then winked at her. "No telling how many miles you've logged on that car by driving out to that ranch at all hours of the day and night."

She could have downplayed the whole thing, but she realized people weren't dumb, especially the ones who knew her so well. The fact was, she was falling for Toby. And that was going to be tough to hide.

But would their happiness last? She hoped so, but she feared they were living in their own little bubble and that reality would eventually intrude.

She just hadn't realized it would happen so soon.

That very afternoon, following her yoga class and Justin's swim lesson—which, thankfully, went off without a hitch!—she entered Toby's kitchen to find him gazing out the window, his hands braced on either side of the sink.

The cordless phone sat on the counter beside the forgotten chicken-and-rice casserole she'd left for him to pop into the oven.

This wasn't good.

Angie told Justin to do his homework and to tell the other kids they'd be eating in thirty minutes. Then she placed the casserole in the preheated oven herself.

When Toby still hadn't moved or otherwise acknowledged her presence, she walked up behind him, slid her arms around his waist and pressed her face to his back. "I'm here if you want to talk about whatever's bothering you."

Toby turned and gathered her into his arms. "I know. And I love having you here. It's just that…" He blew out a sigh. "I got a call from child services. I need to talk to you about it, but not until after the kids go to bed."

The sound of a heated argument rising up in the family room about whose turn it was to use the computer forced Angie to lower her arms and ease out of their embrace.

"Do you want referee duty?" she asked. "Or would you prefer to make the salad?"

"I'd rather putter around in the kitchen alone until I can manage a happy face."

Uh-oh. That phone call hadn't been a good one.

She placed a hand on his cheek, felt the light bristle of his beard, then drew his lips to hers for a quick kiss. "I've got your back, Toby. Don't worry about the kids. I'll keep them busy until dinner is on the table."

Then she walked to the family room, where an old laptop had been set up for the kids to use for homework assignments.

I love having you here, he'd said.

Did that mean he loved *her?* Or that he just loved having her help?

They'd spent so much time together since they'd made love, which would lead Angie to believe that Toby definitely wanted to be with her. Yet, they hadn't had the opportunity for a repeat performance of that magical night, so she was feeling more insecure than she would've liked.

But within minutes of entering the family room, her insecurities disappeared. She was too busy setting time limits on the computer, helping Kylie with her word search and explaining the different biospheres to Brian. Then, of course, she had to explain to Justin that while she didn't mind inviting Mr. Murdock to dinner so he could share more war stories, tonight wasn't a good night for them to have company.

It was funny, though. When she was with Brian, Justin and Kylie, all of the other pressing details in life seemed so inconsequential. These sweet kids needed her and were way more important than her shift at the Superette or her mother's wish to see her married off.

As she herded the children and their freshly washed hands toward the kitchen table, she noticed that Toby had managed to slap on a smile of sorts.

However, he'd also added strawberries to the Caesar salad. Yuck. He knew better than that.

She suspected the telephone call with child services must have really knocked him off-balance because, despite his forced smile and attempts at conversation over dinner, he asked Brian several times what game they'd played during PE today. And then he promised Kylie that she could invite her three best friends to The Cuttery for a beauty makeover day tomorrow, just like Madison Rodriguez had done when it was her birthday.

How was he going to pull that off? Angie had already told him she was having brunch with her mom in Lubbock tomorrow, so she couldn't help him.

She supposed he'd have to ask Jeanne Marie, Deke or one of his sisters to help out, which made Angie feel a little insignificant. But she scolded herself for the crazy thought and shook it off.

What was the matter with her? She deserved a break, didn't she? And besides, shouldn't his mother or his sisters help him out once in a while?

As soon as dinner was over, she handled the bedtime duties alone, while Toby stayed in the kitchen to clean up.

When she finally returned, she stood in the doorway and watched him go through the motions, his mind still clearly on anything but what he was doing, as he wiped the casserole dish over and over again.

"I think that's as dry as it's going to get," she said. "Just leave everything and come with me."

When she reached out her hand to him, he laid the baking dish and towel on the counter. Then he let her lead him outside to the porch, where they took seats on the cushioned patio bench.

While she listened to the ranch sounds at night— cattle lowing, crickets chirping—she waited for him to share what had been weighing on his mind.

Finally, he said, "Ms. Fisk, the kids' case worker, called. Their aunt Barbara isn't ready to leave rehab, but she's been pushing hard to have the children shipped out of state to live with her cousin, a guy who's out on parole and who's never even met them."

The news slammed into Angie like a line drive to

the chest, and her stomach twisted. Toby stood to lose the kids? What would that do to them?

What would it do to *him?*

Oh, God. What would it do to her? She'd grown to love them, to care for them. To want the best for them....

"Did the case worker think that could happen?" she asked. "I mean, they're doing so well."

"She said it was unlikely, but that it could happen. I've read about cases that went badly. And bottom line? I'm just their foster dad. I'm not their blood kin, so I don't have much legal standing."

Angie took his hand in hers, letting him know that she was here for him, that she was worried and hurting, too.

"Did you tell the case worker your concerns?" she asked. "Did you mention how well they're doing, and that uprooting them wouldn't be good for them?"

"I laid out every argument I could think of. And she agreed with me, but her hands are somewhat tied. Apparently, that long-lost cousin in California wants to petition for adoption. And Ms. Fisk thinks the court would rather see the kids in a permanent home than in foster care."

Angie's stomach tossed and turned as she tried to make sense of it all.

"Why would a guy in California suddenly want to adopt three kids he's never even met?" she asked. "That seems like a mighty big step for someone to take."

"I agree. And I hope the judge will consider that question, too. That trust fund could very well be motivating both Barbara and her cousin to seek custody, especially since she knew about my mom's long-lost brother and her connection to the Fortunes. She'd also heard about the incident at the YMCA."

Angie stiffened, and her fingers, still held in the warmth of Toby's hands, grew cold. "You mean she heard about the day I flipped out and the paramedics were called?"

If she'd somehow caused a black mark upon Toby's case, she'd never forgive herself.

"I don't think the incident at the Y had anything to do with Barbara's call to child services and the petition for adoption. But someone in town has been feeding her rumors. And knowing her, the one rumor that she may have heard, the one that may have really caused a stir in her, was the one about the kids' trust fund."

"But you're the trustee. Don't you control the money?"

"That's the problem. I'm the trustee, but the kids' legal guardian is in charge of the monthly payments they receive—and they're substantial. Those classes and all the extras I've been providing them aren't free. Barbara may not know all of the details, but I'm certain she's after whatever money is available to her."

"That's too bad." Angie thought about how her own mother seemed more interested in earning a dollar than in being a stay-at-home mom.

"I'd never planned on using that money for myself," Toby said. "That's why I set it up for their guardian to have control of the monthly income. I didn't mind who had access to it, as long as they were looking out for the kids' best interests. But I hadn't realized Barbara's problems and issues went deeper than her alcohol dependency."

"And now there's her cousin to contend with," Angie added. "Who knows what kind of problems he has. Or what kind of parent or guardian he'd be."

"I've done some online research," Toby said. "And I can't believe any judge in their right mind would think that guy should have custody of them. The last thing they need right now is to move to a home with a man they don't know, a man who's on parole and can't even work at a hospital anymore because of whatever crime he was convicted of. And while I realize he may have paid his debt to society, those poor kids have had enough instability and unhappiness in their lives."

"So what are w…?" Angie cleared her throat, then coughed before she fully pronounced "we." The kids and Toby had become a big part of her life recently, but she wasn't entirely sure where she fit into their lives—at least, in the long run.

She cleared her throat again, then continued with the corrected version of her question. "So what do you plan to do?"

"If it comes to fighting for custody, Ms. Fisk thinks I can win, but she isn't sure. And a 'maybe' isn't good enough for me. It's not a risk I'm willing to take. So I'm giving the court another option. I'm going to talk to an attorney in Lubbock who specializes in family law. And then I'm going to petition for adoption myself. I'll show that I'm much better suited to raise those kids than some ex-con way out in California or a greedy aunt who can't seem to follow the rules in rehab."

While glad that Toby had a game plan and that he

felt more hopeful now than when she'd first arrived, Angie's shoulders slumped and she couldn't stanch the wave of disappointment that swept through her.

She might not have known where she fit into Toby's life, but apparently he did.

He'd just spelled out exactly what he planned to do, saying, "I."

And never once had he used the word *we*.

If there was one thing Angie hated, it was being late when meeting her mother. But she'd tossed and turned all night, thinking long and hard about Toby's dilemma, as well as her own. And she hadn't fallen asleep until almost dawn.

Needless to say, she'd overslept. So she quickly showered, dressed and pulled her hair into a ponytail. She figured she'd apply a quick coat of lipstick when she stopped at the first traffic light in Lubbock.

She'd no more than tossed her purse onto the passenger seat of her car when Mr. Murdock stepped out on his back porch, his cup of coffee steaming in his hands. He was wearing a bright yellow shirt that read Not As Mean, Not As Lean, But Still A Marine.

"Good morning, Mr. Murdock." She gave him a little wave as she slipped behind the wheel and strapped on her seat belt.

"Slow down, Girly." Mr. Murdock took his time as he lumbered down the steps, obviously intent on talking to her.

She'd told him yesterday that she was meeting her mom for brunch this morning. Didn't he realize that if she was even ten minutes late she was in for a lecture even the best mimosa couldn't dull?

When he finally made his way beside her idling car, he asked, "You tell your mama you're living here yet?"

"No, but I promise to do it today." And she would, even if it meant her mother would again offer to put a down payment on a condo in Lubbock for her.

Angie could hear it now. *There's no way I'll tolerate my only child living in some old-timer's run-down granny flat in Horseback Hollow.* In fact, her mom would be scrolling through the online MLS pages before the eggs Benedict arrived.

"Well, that's the thing, Girly. I don't see any need for you to mention that to old Doris."

Old Doris? Angie couldn't help but chuckle. If her mom could hear the eightysomething-year-old veteran refer to her as *old,* she'd be searching the internet for deals on Botox injections.

"Why the change of heart?" Angie asked her landlord. Just last month, Mr. Murdock had insisted that she stand up to her mother and become her own person.

Angie had tried to explain to the competitive man that she was passive-aggressive by nature. And that it was easier to nod her head and then do whatever she wanted to do anyway. So she was surprised that the old marine didn't want her to do battle at brunch today.

"Last night, while I was down at the VFW, Pete told me that the Jones boy was adopting those three kids."

"You shouldn't listen to gossip, Mr. Murdock. Especially from Pete. Wasn't he the one who told you that Ethel Gardiner was as bald as the cue balls in the Two Moon Saloon?"

"Yep. He did."

"And then you pulled on her hair, thinking it was a wig, and she smacked you silly."

"That slap won me five bucks." Mr. Murdock stood tall and puffed out his chest. "Her hair might have been dyed the shade of Pepto-Bismol, but I knew it wasn't no dang wig."

Angie wanted to laugh, but with her foot on the clutch, ready for her to slip the car into Reverse and back out, she was afraid a fit of giggles would cause her to stall the engine.

Besides, she didn't have time to waste getting off on tangents, so she steered the topic back to the original.

"What does Toby adopting those kids have to do with me telling my mother that I rent the granny flat from you?" she asked.

"Well, the way I figure it, since you spend about all your time at his ranch helping him with those young'uns, he'll convince you to move in with him before Old Doris ever finds out you ever lived here."

Thankfully, Mr. Murdock had the grace to turn and walk back to his house so Angie wasn't forced to come up with any sort of reply or denial. Instead, she backed out of the driveway and drove to Lubbock, hoping she didn't get a speeding ticket while she was at it.

As usual, Mr. Murdock had a funny take on things. But there was no way Toby would ask her to move in with him, especially now that he was seeking permanent custody of the kids. In fact, it looked as though their relationship—whatever there was of it—was going to have to take an even bigger backseat to the kids.

But she understood why. And she'd go with the flow. She'd have to deal with her disappointment later.

When she finally arrived at the quaint cottage-style bistro in Lubbock, Angie saw her mother's sedan parked in front. She found an empty space a few shops down the street, yet didn't immediately climb out of the car.

Dealing with Doris Edwards was nothing new. She'd been ignoring her instructions and advice for years. So why did she feel like backing out of the parking space and driving in the opposite direction—as far as she could from Lubbock *and* from Horseback Hollow?

The only thing stopping her from doing so now was a promise she'd made Toby. She'd told him she would pick up the children at the ball field and take them to dinner at The Grill so he could meet with some of his family this afternoon and talk about the adoption plans.

So she couldn't flake on him—or the kids, who would be looking forward to seeing her.

Steeling herself with a deep breath, Angie entered the restaurant and spotted her mom, joining her at a small table in back.

"You finally made it," Doris said. "I thought for sure that old wreck you drive around had broken down somewhere on the highway."

And there was the first insult of the day. But, hey, brunch wouldn't last more than an hour.

"I'm sorry I'm late," Angie said. "How are you, Mom?"

"I've never been better. And you'd know that if you came to see me more."

Insult number two.

"I wish I could come to town more often, but I've been busy lately."

"So I've heard. I talked to Ethel Gardiner on Monday. And she said that you've been spending a lot of time with Toby Fortune Jones and those kids he has running around his house."

Angie crossed her arms, suddenly not the least bit sorry about Mr. Murdock's bet with Pete. Ethel Gardiner deserved to have her pink locks tugged after spreading gossip.

"For the record," Angie said, "Toby's an amazing guy. Not many men would give up so much to take care of three children who weren't their own."

"That's just it," Doris argued. "Those kids *aren't* his own. It's unnatural. I mean, maybe if he used some of his family money and spent more time making something out of that ranch of his and less time playing daddy, he could be the right man for you."

Angie wanted to tell her mother that Toby didn't have any family money, but it really wasn't any of her business. So instead she signaled the waitress and ordered a much-needed cappuccino.

She normally would've spent twenty minutes reading every detailed item on the menu and trying to decide what to order. But since she wanted to get out of this restaurant as quickly as possible, she pointed to the frittata special—which was the first thing listed on the menu.

Her mother ordered plain yogurt, and Angie wondered why the woman would even bother coming out to eat if that was all she was going to have.

"You know," Angie said, "if you drove out to the

ranch and spent some time with Toby and the kids, you'd see things differently."

Had Angie actually suggested that? What would Toby say? He might claim to be easygoing, but having her mom around would probably be the kiss of death for their relationship—or whatever it was they had.

"Your defensive response is telling," Doris said.

"Telling?" How could it tell Doris anything when Angie didn't know what she was feeling herself?

"It sounds like you're trying to sell me on a ready-made family. You're not, are you? I mean, look at your history. You've avoided any kind of commitment in the past—and not just when it comes to relationships."

Angie couldn't argue with that.

"Besides," Doris said, "if you can't commit one hundred percent to those kids, then you shouldn't waste your time with their foster dad. It wouldn't be fair, especially if those children have lost as many people as everyone says they have."

Angie didn't normally see eye to eye with her mom, but those last words resonated loud and clear.

She didn't want to give anyone false hope, especially those kids.

"Plus, dear, you were meant to be so much more than just a mother."

Was she? She'd always thought that she was destined for more. After all, Doris had been telling her that for years. But she could still hear Jeanne Marie's words, still feel the way they'd warmed her heart.

...you're more than qualified to do my *job.*

Angie had been good at it, too. And she liked the kids. She'd even turned down some afternoon shifts at the Superette so that she could help Toby more with the carpooling.

But the Mama Angie gig had only been going on for a couple of weeks. Could she continue doing it for the next ten or fifteen years?

And did she even want to?

When the waitress brought their breakfast, Angie stared at the frittata placed in front of her. Why hadn't she ordered the stuffed French toast instead?

For some reason she found herself retreating back to her usual on-the-fence mode.

Was she up to the job of raising children?

Talk about long-term commitments.

What if the kids bonded with her, and then she skipped out on them?

Or maybe even worse, what if she stuck it out, like her mother had done when Angie had been growing up, and the decision to stay in an unhappy situation only made her life, as well as those of everyone around her, miserable?

No, in this case, her mother had called it right. Angie had never been able to commit to anything up until now. And those children needed stability in their lives more than anything.

Of course, Toby had never given her any reason to believe he envisioned her as a part of his long-term family plan. And the fact that he hadn't lanced something soft and fragile inside.

In what ways had Toby found her lacking?

Certainly not as a lover—or as a teammate, baby-sitter or friend.

But did he question her ability to make a lasting commitment to him and the kids? If so, she couldn't blame him for that. Because as much as she'd come to care for that precious little family, she had those same worries herself.

"I know you've never taken my advice in the past," Doris said. "And it's no secret that you pretend to listen— and that you think I'm pushy."

For some reason, Angie couldn't let that one go without commenting. "Listen, Mom. I love you. And I appreciate the fact that you believe you have my best interests at heart. But this is my life, not yours. You may have made some bad choices in the past, but they were yours to make—and yours to live with. Right or wrong, I intend to do the same thing. If you want to offer a bit of advice, that's fine. But then drop it. Please."

Doris sat there for a moment, then cleared her throat. "I'm sorry, Angie. Believe it or not, I really don't mean to interfere. I'll try to be more respectful of you in the future. And I'll be supportive of whatever you decide to do—even if it means going out to the ranch for a visit."

"Thank you. And for the record, I truly care for Toby and those kids. I actually love them. But deciding what to do about that isn't a simple decision for me to make. And no matter what I choose to do, I'll do it with my eyes and my heart wide open, knowing that if I make the wrong decision, if I end up hurt or disappointed in the long run, then so be it."

Doris placed her napkin in her lap, signaling it was time to eat and to put unpleasant matters behind them. "Since you understand the importance and are giving it a great deal of thought, I can respect that. So I'll drop the subject. I just hope that you will be able to make that decision quickly."

Her mother had never been more right.

Angie was facing the most critical decision she'd ever had to make—one that could prove to be life-changing and heartbreaking. And one she couldn't afford to stew about.

But instead of only having to consider the effects of her choice on her own life, her own heart, she had to consider what it would do to three children and to Toby, as well.

That being said, she really had to follow her heart, even if it was breaking. And that meant there was only one possible choice.

She had to step back and let them go.

And the sooner she told Toby the better.

Chapter Eleven

Toby's meeting with his family had gone even better than he'd hoped. When he'd laid out his dilemma and his plan, they'd all agreed to support him in a full-scale custody battle—if it should come to that—and in his attempt to adopt Brian, Justin and Kylie.

The only concern that had come up was the cost of legal fees, which could get expensive, but Toby had already talked at length to Jake Gleason, the attorney who'd drawn up the trust. So he was able to explain to his family that he, as the trustee, was allowed to tap into the principal at his discretion for any unexpected needs the kids might have. He'd also been able to assure them that securing a permanent home qualified as such a need.

So now Toby was on his way to The Grill. He intended to have a heart-to-heart talk with Angie while the kids played in the arcade. He wasn't looking forward to it, but he had to do it.

Over the past twenty-four hours, he'd been preoccupied with thoughts of the custody hearing and the adoption, but not so much that he hadn't sensed a very subtle difference in Angie. And he'd picked up on it again in the distant tone in her voice when they'd talked on the phone earlier.

He sensed that she was withdrawing from him, just as he'd suspected she would. And he really couldn't blame her. His life had taken a sudden and complicated turn, one their budding relationship wasn't prepared to handle.

Asking her to babysit or to fix Kylie's hair was one thing, but assuming that she'd want to take on even more responsibility or to actually become a permanent part of his and the children's lives was something completely different.

For one thing, she was still trying to find herself and her way in the world. How could he ask her to take on a burden she clearly wasn't ready for? Besides, she might want to have her own kids someday, and a large family was... Well, it was probably more than a woman who'd grown up as an only child would ever consider.

On top of that, they hadn't been dating very long.

Dating? He couldn't even call it that. One amazing night of lovemaking, no matter how amazing it might have been, wasn't the kind of romantic relationship Angie deserved. Not when the bulk of their time together was spent dealing with sick kids, spilled milk and squabbles over whose turn it was to use the laptop or the TV remote.

Heck, Toby had never even taken her out on a real

date, had never provided her with candlelight and roses. There'd been no nights on the town, no holding hands in the movie theater or dancing until dawn.

So allowing things to continue in the way they'd been going wasn't fair to her.

Knowing Angie, she was probably trying to figure out how to end things between them without hurting or disappointing the kids. So Toby would just have to make things easier on her. And, in the long run, he'd make things easier on all of them.

While the kids played in the arcade, oblivious to the custody battle that loomed, Toby would thank Angie for all she'd done for him. Then he'd let her off the hook, making the decision for her. If she wanted to stick around for dinner, they'd have one last meal together, then she'd go her way, and he and the kids would go theirs.

It sounded easy enough. He just hoped his voice didn't crack and reveal the ache in his heart that set in whenever he thought about her walking out of his life for good.

When Toby arrived at The Grill and spotted Angie's Toyota in the parking lot, his heart skipped a beat, and his breathing stalled. She'd probably been here awhile, since he was ten minutes later than he'd told her he'd be.

Yet he continued to sit in his truck, his hands on the steering wheel, wishing there was another way around what he had to do, but knowing there wasn't. Finally, he mustered his courage and opened the driver's door to let himself out. Then he headed for the front entrance.

When he stepped inside The Grill, he was met by Bonnie Sue Hillman, a petite blonde waitress.

"Angie is in the big booth in back," Bonnie Sue

said, "and the kids are in the arcade, going through quarters like crazy."

"Thanks. Have they ordered yet?"

Bonnie Sue laughed. "Angie's only been here for about fifteen minutes, and it takes her a lot longer than that just to study the menu."

As Toby made his way to the booth where Angie sat, another waitress stopped at her table. She said something to Angie and nodded. Then she whipped out her pad and pencil.

Toby approached, just as Angie said, "Brian will have the cheeseburger—well-done, no onions, lettuce or pickles. But he'd like extra tomatoes. And can you bring a side of mustard for his fries?"

As the waitress made note of it, Angie added, "Justin would like the corn dog, but instead of fries, he'll have onion rings with a side of ranch dressing. Kylie wants the grilled cheese with American—not cheddar. And can you please ask the cook to cut it into four triangles? If not, I can do that. She'd also like a bowl of strawberries—if you have them. When Toby gets here, he'll want the double bacon cheeseburger, fried pickles and a peanut-butter milk shake. He can share the onion rings with Justin. And I'll have the patty melt on rye and an iced tea with lemon."

Bonnie Sue, who'd followed Toby to the booth with a handful of menus, blew out a little whistle. "That's gotta be some kind of record. You'd think Angie's been ordering food for you guys for years."

It sure seemed that way. She'd picked up on a lot of their habits in a few short weeks. But then again, they didn't call her Little Miss Google for nothing.

Still, it tugged at his heart that the woman who'd

fallen into his life seemed to have somehow picked *him* up after that fall.

Angie looked up and spotted Toby. "Oh, you're here. I'm sorry. I probably shouldn't have ordered for you."

"No, that's fine. I'm glad you did." He slid into the booth and placed his hat on the seat beside him.

"How did it go?" she asked.

"Great. My family is behind me one hundred percent."

"I knew they would be."

Toby studied his hands, which rested on the table.

"Is something wrong?" she asked. "Do you want to talk about it before the kids come back?"

All right. This was the opening he needed. Now all he had to do was form the words.

He took a deep, fortifying breath. "Things will probably get pretty intense over the next few weeks and months."

"I know."

He paused a beat, then pressed on. "I realize you didn't sign on for all of this. And I want you to know that I understand. At this point, you can bow out gracefully before anyone gets hurt."

There. He'd said it.

Now all he had to do was wait and see what she would do with the ball he'd lobbed into her court.

Angie hadn't been sure how to tell Toby that she'd decided to back off, that she needed some space and time to herself. Then he'd broached the subject himself.

Not only that, he'd practically spelled it all out for

her, making it easy. But now that he'd given her a free pass…

Well…was taking a step back what she really wanted?

In truth, she hadn't been ready to walk away yet. But because she was afraid she'd change her mind down the road, which would devastate the kids, she'd thought it would be best to do it now.

And apparently, Toby felt the same way.

Yet now that he was cutting her loose, she felt an incredible sense of loss and fear that she stood to lose everything she'd ever wanted or needed if she didn't speak up…

Speak up and say what? That she didn't want to completely bow out?

That, in fact, she might not want to bow out at all?

"You're not saying anything," Toby said. "What are you thinking?"

"That I'd planned to take a step back and give you guys time to yourselves, but not because of the problems you're facing."

"Then why?"

"It's complicated."

Toby leaned forward. "I'm going to fight to keep Brian, Justin and Kylie. So things aren't temporary anymore. I'm making a commitment to them—one I hope the courts will make permanent. And as much as the kids—and I—would like you to be a part of that, I wouldn't even think of asking you to stick around for the long haul. It would be asking too much, and it wouldn't be fair."

Good. That was what she'd wanted to explain to him.

But the way he'd said it, the way he'd implied that it was just him and the kids from here on out—a family through thick and thin—made her feel as though she was the odd man out. And she wasn't so sure she wanted to be on the outside looking in.

She lifted her eyes, caught his gaze zeroing in on hers. Glossy. Intense.

His words told her he was letting her go and that he thought it was for the best.

Okay, she got that. But his pained expression said something entirely different to her heart.

Or did she just want to read something into all the emotions she saw brewing in his eyes?

"What's the matter?" he asked. "I thought you'd be relieved to have an opportunity to ease out of this relationship."

She should be. She'd come here intending to end things between them after dinner, then return to her own little corner of the world—the part-time job at the Superette, the twenty hours a week at Redmond-Fortune Air, the small little granny flat behind Mr. Murdock's house that she called home....

But was that cute little granny flat where she really called home?

Not when she woke up each morning in her own bed, thinking about Toby, seeing his face, hearing his voice. And whenever she thought about going home, it was always to the Double H, where Toby, the kids and one big mess or another always awaited her.

Come to think of it, no matter where she was— brunch with her mom, the Superette or at the airfield, her thoughts revolved around that precious, ragtag family. Even in her spare time, she planned meals she thought they'd like to eat and worked out better ways to balance their busy after-school schedules.

Just this morning, when she'd fixed her hair before her shift at the store, she'd wondered if Kylie was wearing the new headband Toby had bought her to use on days Angie wasn't there to braid her hair. She'd also wanted to tell Justin to practice his spelling words one more time and to remind Brian not to forget his backpack.

She'd gone so far as to pick up the phone to call Toby and offer her suggestions, but she'd been afraid that she was getting way too involved, especially if she was going to distance herself.

But as she looked at Toby now, as she saw his anguished expression, as she realized how difficult this was for him...

It was breaking his heart, and for that reason, it was breaking hers, too.

He was all on his own and facing a custody battle, one he might lose. But that wasn't the only thing hurting him.

Call it a zany sixth sense, but Angie could see it as plain as the summer sun at high noon. He was struggling with letting her go.

And she was struggling, too—right along with him.

All she wanted to do was to make his pain go away, to settle his fear, to strengthen his resolve.

And for some crazy reason, she didn't even question the fact that she might be wrong in her assumption about what he was feeling for her.

The solution to the problem, to *their* problem, had

never seemed so clear or so simple. All she had to do was to follow her heart.

Without a thought to the repercussions, the words rolled out of her mouth as loud and clear as the church bells on Sunday morning. "Toby, I think we should get married."

He blinked, and his lips parted. "What did you say?"

"Those kids need a loving, two-parent home. And you and I are the ones who can provide it for them. I want us to be a family. And if we go before the court together, I don't think the judge will turn us down."

"You mean you'd marry me because of the kids?"

Angie laughed. "I want to marry you because I love you. And because I love the kids, I want us to be a family."

Toby reached across the table and took her hand in his. "You love me?"

"Yes." How could she not? He was everything a woman could ever want in a man—loving, loyal, a family man... And he was the most handsome man in all of Texas—if not the whole world.

"Are you sure about that?" he asked. "You're not going to change your mind?"

"I've always known that when the perfect choice came along, I'd know it and that I'd jump on it. And that's what I'm doing. When I'm with you and the kids, I don't feel the least bit insecure or indecisive or flighty. I feel in control, at home, and..." She paused, realizing that was one word she needed to hear Toby say himself.

"And what?" Toby asked. "I hope you feel loved,

because I'm crazy about you." He slid around to her side of the booth and slipped his arm around her. "And I'm going to spend the rest of my life proving to you just how much."

Angie leaned into him. "I must admit, I felt loved and cherished on Saturday night."

He brushed a kiss on her cheek. "Honey, if we weren't out in public, I'd make you feel loved and cherished right now."

She laughed. "Something tells me our private times together, as nice as they'll be, aren't going to be easy to find. But I'll put some thought into it and figure out something."

"One thing I can do is to call Stacey and ask if she knows any reliable sitters we can hire on a regular basis. We're going to set aside one day a week as date night. I'd also like to plan some romantic weekend getaways."

Angie's heart swelled until she thought it might burst wide open. "I'm going to like being married to you, Toby."

"I'm glad, because the more I think about it, the more I like the idea of being married to you."

"It's too bad the junior college doesn't offer a crash course in motherhood," she said. "There's a lot I need to learn. Maybe I should ask your mom to tutor me."

"You're doing just fine. You've picked up plenty already."

"I'm not sure about that."

"Oh, no? You know which girls in Brian's class think he's cute and how many breaths Justin takes when he swims the length of the YMCA pool. It took you all of fifteen seconds to figure out how to juggle the timing of Kylie's gymnastics lesson and still get the boys to baseball practice on time. You're a natural—and a fast learner. You've also come to know me pretty well."

She smiled and bumped his shoulder with hers. "Oh, yeah?"

"You can read my mood like nobody's business. You knew that I really wanted to beg you to stay with me and the kids, even though I was trying to do the gentlemanly thing and give you a way out. And, maybe even more importantly, you know how to set my blood on fire."

She leaned in and gave him a long, heated kiss that could have set The Grill on fire if he hadn't drawn back.

Toby ran his finger along her lips. "But you need to know something. No matter what happens with the kids, even if I lose them, I still want you for my wife."

"We won't lose them," Angie said. "I've set my heart on it."

For the first time since Ms. Fisk had returned his call and told him Barbara had moved forward with her plan, Toby began to relax. With Angie in his corner, how could he lose?

Before either of them could comment further, the kids dashed back to the table announcing their high scores and asking for more quarters.

"What do you think?" Angie asked Toby. "Should we tell them?"

Justin pressed in front of his brother and sister. "Tell us what?"

"Angie and I are getting married," Toby said.

"No kidding?" Brian asked. "Sweet."

"Woo-hoo!" Justin shouted, drawing the other diners' attention to their table.

Kylie clapped her hands and gave a little jump. "Can I be in the wedding?"

"Absolutely," Angie said. "You're all going to be in the wedding. We wouldn't have it any other way."

"So when is it?" Brian asked.

"We'll have to wait at least three days," Angie said. "That's Texas law."

Toby chuckled. "I suppose you picked that trivial piece of info up at one of your temp jobs?"

"As a matter of fact, I spent a few weeks working at a bridal shop in Vicker's Corners."

Miss Google strikes again.

"So how soon can I call you my wife?" Toby asked.

Angie tossed him a flirtatious grin. "How does next Saturday sound?"

"That long, huh?" He slipped his arm around her again and drew her close. "Saturday is fine with me. But don't you think you'll need more time to plan a wedding?"

"Yes, but I'd like to keep things simple. You may not believe this, but I can practically see it all unfolding in my mind."

"You're right. That *is* hard to believe, but I don't doubt it." He leaned over and kissed her again.

"Hey," Justin said. "Before you guys start smooching again, can you look and see if you have any more quarters?"

Toby laughed, then dug into his pocket and pulled out several. "Take these."

When the kids dashed off, Toby turned his attention back to Angie. "So you're not going to drag your feet and make me wait while you stew over bridal magazines and reception venues?"

"No, I won't have to. When I make up my mind, and my heart's in it, I don't drag my feet. I can tell you right now that I'd like to be married in your parents' backyard. And that I want Stacey and Delaney to be my bridesmaids. I've never had sisters, so I'm looking forward to having two right off the bat."

"I'm sure they'll be happy about that."

"Good. Then since we're both on the same page, I don't see a problem."

"Neither do I."

Well, other than having to wait until next Saturday to make love with her again. But he was going to work very hard at getting her alone before that.

"I don't suppose you've thought about a guest list," he said. "Saturday won't give us time to send out invitations."

"We'll keep it simple—mostly family, if that's okay. But with it being so soon, we'll have to call and invite people."

"I'd like my brother Chris to be there, but that's going to be tricky."

"Because of the hard feelings within the family?" she asked.

"Yes. Chris has always been both a black sheep and a lone wolf. I've understood that and known when to give him his space. After things blew sky-high, I knew he needed to do some airing out. So I gave him the time he needed, figuring that he'd contact me when he was ready to talk and move back into the fold."

"So will you call him?" Angie asked. "You could use the wedding as an excuse."

"It might be best to extend the invitation through Sawyer. That way I'm respecting his decision to distance himself from Horseback Hollow and from the rest of the family. Yet it's also a way to let him know that I still love him and want a relationship with him. I have a feeling he'll reach out to me at that point, even if he doesn't come."

"Do you think he'll stay away?"

"I hope not, but Chris has always had to do things his way. In the meantime, my dad will need to do some bending, too. So if I want to see any fences getting mended, I'd better start working on him."

"If anyone can talk some sense into your dad, I'll bet you can." Angie gave him a kiss. "Now let's get busy. I have a lot of work to do—and nine days doesn't give me much time."

She was right. But when it came to waiting for Angie to move into the ranch and become his wife in every sense of the word, nine days seemed way too long.

Toby had an appointment to meet with his new attorney in Lubbock on Monday at eleven o'clock. So. while he was in the city, he decided to stop by the real-estate office where Doris Edwards worked.

Needless to say, she was surprised to see him.

"Do you have a couple of minutes?" he asked.

"Certainly." She led him down the hall to a small break room. "Would you like a cup of coffee?"

"No, thanks. I can't stay long, but I have a question for you."

"What's that?"

"I'd like to ask for Angie's hand in marriage."

Doris sat up a little straighter. "That's a bit of a surprise—and a little old-fashioned. What if I were to tell you no?"

"We'd get married anyway. I just thought I'd pay you the respect you deserve—and to ask that you do the same for us."

"I see." Doris sat back in her seat. "So have you proposed to Angie yet?"

"Actually, it was her idea. She's the one who first popped the question." A slow smile tugged at his lips. "She's going to call you when she gets off work today and talk to you about it."

"Have you set a date?"

"Saturday."

"So soon?" Doris stiffened. "Are you eloping?"

"We're going to get married at my parents' ranch. We're only inviting family and a few close friends, although I suspect it won't be as small as it sounds."

Doris perked up. "Will the Fortunes from Red Rock be attending?"

"They'll be invited, as well as those from Atlanta and the United Kingdom. But with it being such short notice, I'm not sure who'll be able to make it."

"In that case, don't you think it would be better to wait at least a month? That way, you'll have more time to plan a nicer event. I might even be able to get the *Lubbock Avalanche-Journal* to run a spread in the society pages."

"We don't want to wait."

"Oh, dear. She's not pregnant, is she?"

Toby groaned inwardly. Doris Edwards was certainly going to be a trial, but Angie was worth it.

"No, she's not pregnant. But don't worry—even though we only have a few days to plan, the wedding is going to be nice. My entire family is pitching in, and we'd like you to be as involved as you want to be."

"Of course I'd like to be included." Doris began to click her manicured nails on the table—plotting and planning, no doubt. "I'll also need to purchase a new dress to wear." She bit down on her bottom lip, then looked at him with hope-filled eyes. "Do you think your aunt Josephine May Fortune Chesterfield will come all the way from England? Goodness, I'll bet the cost of *that* flight will be incredibly expensive."

Toby reached out and placed his hand over his future mother-in-law's, stopping her from fidgeting. "Listen, Doris. There are a few things we need to get straight. I may be a Fortune by blood, and while my ranch is doing just fine and I'm financially stable, I'm not wealthy by any means. And I probably never will be. But I love your daughter with all my heart. We may never have the money that some of my family members have, but in everything that matters, Angie and I are rich beyond measure."

Doris smiled. "I understand. But you can't help me for being a little starstruck. I mean, the Chesterfields are almost royals in the U.K."

Toby didn't know about that, but at least Doris seemed to support his and Angie's union.

"Do you think it would be all right if I stopped by to see Jeanne Marie and Deke after I get off work today?" Doris asked. "I'd love to offer my services—and to do whatever I can to offset the cost of the wedding. I'm not rich, either, but I did set aside some cash for my baby girl's big day."

Toby didn't dare tell her that Sawyer had already offered to do the same thing. Or that Sawyer's dad, James Marshall Fortune, had agreed to pay for their honeymoon in San Antonio, the flight courtesy of Redmond-Fortune Air.

Doris might accept that Toby wasn't as rich as some of the other Fortunes, but she'd certainly place a boatload of value on his family connections.

"I'm sure my parents would be glad to have you stop by this evening," Toby said, as he stood, preparing to leave.

His talk with Doris had gone better than he'd hoped. She seemed to be looking forward to the wedding.

He just hoped she wouldn't place any unnecessary stress on Angie, especially on their special day.

Angie, Stacey and Delaney were going to shop for dresses in Vicker's Corners on Tuesday afternoon. Angie's mom, who'd been both supportive and excited about the upcoming ceremony, was coming along, too.

Who would have guessed that Doris would actually be looking forward to her role as mother of the bride?

Angie had a feeling her excitement might have something to do with knowing that there would be quite a few Fortunes present and that one of Toby's handsome brothers would be walking her down the aisle. But either way, it would make the day go by a whole lot smoother.

Her mom was also planning to purchase the bridal gown, which was nice. And as long as Stacey and Delaney were there to prevent her from going tulle-crazy, it should work out okay.

Before driving to the bridal shop to meet everyone, Angie stopped at Mr. Murdock's house to tell him about the upcoming wedding and to let him know that she'd be moving out in less than a week.

"So that Fortune Jones boy has finally talked some sense into you, did he?"

Angie smiled at the old man she'd grown so fond of in the past couple of months. "Yes, he certainly did."

Mr. Murdock turned and headed to the lamp table, where he kept his telephone.

"What are you doing?" she asked, a little disappointed that he'd walked off while she was still sharing the news of the biggest and best decision she'd ever made in her life.

"I need to call Pete," he said.

"Your VFW buddy? Why?"

"Because I told him you'd be tying the knot by the end of the month. But he thought those young'uns would scare you off. So now Pete owes me five bucks and two of his lucky bingo cards."

"Oh, no. Please tell me you didn't make a bet on my love life."

"Girly," Mr. Murdock said with a big ole grin, "I'd bet on you any day of the week."

Coming from him, that was a huge compliment.

He picked up a glass of amber-colored liquid from the table. "Can I get you some Scotch?"

"No, thanks. And you shouldn't be drinking it, either. You really need to cut back. Remember what your doctor said?"

He glanced at the glass, scrunched his face as though he was really giving it some thought, then returned the drink to the table.

She didn't think he'd go so far as to pour it out, though. She suspected that he was going to finish it as soon as she left.

"Listen," she said. "There's something else, Mr. Murdock. I'd like to ask you to be in our wedding."

"Huh?" He scrunched his craggy face, as if thinking it over, then pointed an arthritic finger at her. "I know you young kids today are all okay with this gender-role-reversal business, and I'll go ahead and be your brides-man or man of honor or whatever you equal-rights hippies are calling it nowadays. But I ain't wearing no pink tuxedo."

Angie suddenly wished she'd accepted the glass of Scotch so she could lift it to her face and camouflage her twitching lips. "I wasn't asking you to stand up with me in the bridal party, Mr. Murdock."

"No?"

"I want you to walk me down the aisle."

Chapter Twelve

Saturday finally dawned, bringing a cloudless sky, a lazy breeze and a buzz of excitement. It was a perfect day for a wedding.

As two o'clock approached, the guests began to arrive and mingle. Toby stood off to the side, taking it all in and feeling as though he'd been blessed beyond measure.

He surveyed the once-familiar yard, which had morphed into a festive, ranch-style setting for the outdoor ceremony, thanks to the rented lattice gazebo, the white chairs lined up on the freshly mowed lawn and the small stage where the DJ was setting up his equipment next to the portable dance floor.

Marcos and Wendy Mendoza, who planned to open The Hollows Cantina at the end of June, had volunteered to cater the event as a wedding gift. They'd flown in from Red Rock two days before and were already laying out their spread on the linen-draped tables that had been adorned with the bouquets of flowers Angie and his sisters had created yesterday.

Come to find out his new bride had once worked for a florist in Vicker's Corners. With all the random skills Angie had acquired at her temp jobs, she was proving to be surprisingly handy.

As Toby marveled at all the work everyone had done in order to get the family homestead ready and decorated for a wedding, he shook his head in amazement.

Last night, his parents had hosted a rehearsal dinner with many of the Fortunes in attendance. Not all of his newfound relatives had been able to drop everything and come to Horseback Hollow, but quite a few from Red Rock and Atlanta had actually made the trip. Even Amelia Fortune Chesterfield had flown in from England.

But there was one family member noticeably missing—his brother Chris.

Toby had planned to talk to Sawyer, but a few minutes ago, his cousin had stepped away from the crowd to take a phone call. When Toby saw that Sawyer had put away his cell, he crossed the yard and made his way toward the man whose charter service had been busy all week flying guests into town.

"You're just the guy I wanted to see," Sawyer said.

"Same here. Did you talk to my brother?"

Sawyer reached into his lapel and pulled out what appeared to be a greeting card. "He asked me to give you this before the wedding."

Toby studied the pale blue envelope, then slipped his finger under the flap and tore it open. After removing the card, he read the printed words that wished the bride and groom all the best as they started their lives together. It was signed: Love, Chris.

Sawyer again reached into his lapel. This time, he withdrew a white business envelope. "He also wanted me to give you this. Open it."

Toby did, finding ten crisp one-hundred dollar bills inside. The amount of the gift was staggering, and while he appreciated his brother's generosity, he actually would have preferred just the card and having Chris attend the wedding in person. But he wouldn't mention his disappointment to Sawyer.

Instead, he said, "Chris must be doing well in Red Rock."

"I think so. And he's sorry he couldn't be here, but he figured, under the circumstances, his presence would only put a damper on your special day. And that's not the kind of wedding memory he wanted you and Angie to have."

As much as Toby would like to argue, Chris had a point.

"He also said to tell you that, if you ever need anything, he's just a phone call away."

Toby nodded, knowing that his brother's heart was softening. And that it was in the right place. "Thanks for being the go-between, Sawyer. I really appreciate it."

"I just wish I could have done more to help smooth things over."

"He'll come around. Eventually." Toby folded the envelope in half and slid it into his own lapel pocket.

"Would you look at all of this?" Sawyer lifted his hand and gestured to the decorated ranch and to the happy people milling about. "Who would have guessed that you and Angie could have pulled off something like this so quickly?"

"She worked her tail off," Toby said. "We both did. But we had a lot of help. And we appreciate your contribution, too."

"Flying you to San Antonio for your honeymoon was the least Laurel and I could do. I just wish you and Angie were able to stay for more than a few days."

"Our attorney said we need to demonstrate that we're the best caretakers for the children, so we didn't want it to look like we were ditching them the first chance we got. Four days will be enough."

Plus, they would miss the kids while they were gone. Maybe, in late summer, the five of them could take a family honeymoon to Six Flags.

"When my dad offered to pay for your hotel room," Sawyer said, "he hoped you'd choose a more exotic locale for your honeymoon."

"San Antonio is a beautiful city. Besides, we won't have to leave the state. And if we need to, we can get home fairly quick."

"That makes sense."

"But speaking of San Antonio," Toby said, "it's only a short drive from there to Red Rock. I think Angie and I will rent a car and stop by the Fortune Foundation to see Chris while we're in the area. It's time I talked to him in person."

That family rift had gone on too long. And it was time to mend fences.

"Uh-oh," Sawyer said. "You're being paged."

Toby scanned the grounds and spotted Jude, who was motioning for him, indicating it was time to get this show on the road.

"I'll talk to you later," Toby said. "Thanks again for everything."

Sawyer placed a hand on Toby's shoulder and gave it an affectionate squeeze. "Congratulations, cousin. I hope you and Angie will be as happy as Laurel and I are."

"I'm sure we will be."

Toby crossed the yard, then took his place at the gazebo, near the minister. His brothers—minus Chris—and Brian followed behind him, lining up at his side.

Just as Angie had promised, the kids all played a special part in the ceremony. Brian took pride in his role as a junior groomsman, while Justin felt honored to be the ring bearer, especially since it had been explained that his was the most important job of all. And Kylie, of course, was delighted to be the flower girl.

Now all the hard work and last night's practice was coming into play.

As the music began, signaling the start of the processional, Justin started down the aisle, balancing the small white satin pillow that had been in the Jones family for generations in one hand and tugging Kylie's flower-bearing arm with the other.

The guests laughed at the struggling pair of red-heads who eventually took their positions in front of the minister.

"There's still flowers left in my basket," Kylie stage-whispered to Justin.

With that, her brother snatched the basket out of her grasp and emptied it, dumping rose petals all over Toby's black cowboy boots. Then he pointed to the pile and smiled. "Now when Angie walks down the aisle, she'll know where she's supposed to end up."

Several of the guests covered their mouths to hold back their giggles. But apparently Doris Edwards didn't find it funny, because she turned her "grand-dame of Lubbock" eyes on anyone who seemed to be laughing at her daughter's expense.

Doris hadn't made it out to the Double H for a visit yet, but she'd purchased Angie's wedding dress and had paid the extra fees for the rush alterations. So she was definitely coming around.

Of course, she'd been on her best behavior last night at the rehearsal dinner. She'd also just happened to bring along some colorful brochures of houses and various other properties she had listed for sale. Apparently Toby's soon-to-be mother-in-law was in her element socializing and networking with his Fortune family members.

Next in the procession came the bridesmaids—Julia Tierney, who was engaged to Liam, and Gabi Mendoza, Jude's fiancée, followed by Toby's sisters, Stacey and Delaney.

But all thoughts of in-laws and family members

dissipated in the light afternoon breeze when the first chords of the bridal march were played.

The moment Toby spotted his bride, his breath caught at the sight of her. She wore a strapless, form-fitting satin gown that hugged her womanly curves, and when she flashed him a dazzling smile his lungs filled with so much pride he could have floated to the moon and back.

As she began her walk down the aisle on Mr. Murdock's arm, he realized his life was about to change in the most amazing way ever. And he couldn't wait until they became one—from this day forward, now and forever…

When Angie reached the gazebo, Mr. Murdock, who wore his much-too-snug dress uniform, handed her off to Toby.

"Who gives this woman away?" the minister asked.

The retired marine, who'd stepped back to his place of honor in the front row, drew up to his full five feet four inches, placed his hand on Doris's shoulder and roared out in his best drill-instructor voice, "Her mother and I do."

Toby had to bite back a laugh when Angie's mom leaned away and looked at Amelia Fortune Chesterfield, who represented the British Fortunes, as if wanting to silently communicate that she wasn't even remotely related to the elderly man.

Yet when Angie slipped her hand in Toby's, when she gazed into his eyes, all thoughts of laughter ceased. He was about to marry the most beautiful, loving woman in the whole world. And when she smiled back at him, he didn't think he could say "I do" fast enough.

Angie had never been happier. And her confident smile lasted all through the minister's opening words and continued through their vows. She'd just married the most perfect man ever made, and she'd never been more certain of a decision in her life.

The moment they were finally pronounced man and wife and Toby kissed her, the Hemings kids, dressed in their bridal finery, let loose with whoops, hoots and whistles.

If anyone thought the outburst was out of place, it would be her mother. But when Toby's family joined in with cheers and applause of their own, Angie couldn't see how her mom could possibly complain.

As the happy guests finally quieted down, the minister said, "May I be the first to introduce you to Mr. and Mrs. Toby Fortune Jones."

Again, the applause and cheers rang out.

The music began, signaling it was time to proceed back down the aisle, and Angie blew a kiss to her mom.

As soon as she and Toby had cleared the last row of chairs, he asked, "Are you glad it's over?"

"The ceremony? Yes. But our lives are just beginning, and I've never been happier."

"Neither have I."

"For the record," she admitted, "I'm looking forward to saying goodbye to our guests and having you all to myself, though."

Toby stroked his fingers along the delicate satin

on her back. "That dress is beautiful, and it couldn't look better on any other bride. But I can't wait to get you out of it."

As he brushed a kiss on her lips, and the photographer snapped another picture, Angie wholeheartedly agreed. The wedding night couldn't come quickly enough.

While the photographer went to gather up all the family members for some formal shots, Toby pulled her behind an elm tree, not far from the tree fort.

"Listen, about our honeymoon," he started.

Oh, no. Would they have to cancel? Had something come up with the kids or the babysitting arrangement? Oh, well. They'd just have to make do. She refused to be disappointed on the happiest day of her life.

"Since we'll be so close to Red Rock," Toby said, "I thought we could take one afternoon to visit Chris."

"That's a great idea."

Toby told her about the card and the monetary gift. "I think it's time to find out how he's doing and how he's feeling about things. He isn't the black sheep some people see him as."

Angie glanced down at the platinum band sparkling on her finger. She was Toby's wife now—and as much a part of the Fortune clan as everyone else. So she was doubly invested in making sure all members were happy and getting along.

"Maybe Chris would just like to get to know his uncle better," she said.

"You might be right. But he's probably also attracted to a new and different lifestyle. He went to college, so he has ideas on new ways to do things. And my dad's an old-school sort. Chris doesn't think Dad respects him. And my dad thinks Chris has gotten too big for his britches. In reality, they're probably both right."

"Do you think you can help them make peace with each other?"

"I'm sure going to try."

A snapping twig sounded, and the photographer called out. "Here they are."

As the rest of the family followed behind, the photographer asked them to gather in the shade of the tree, but he continued to snap random shots at the crowd anyway.

"Is this everyone?" the photographer asked.

No, it wasn't everyone, but that was okay. With all the couples who'd been hooking up lately, there was bound to be another wedding and reception soon. And they could get a bigger group photo then.

Jeanne Marie moved in next to Toby and, between smiles for the camera, whispered, "I'm so sorry Chris isn't here. I feel as though a part of me is missing."

Angie's heart ached for her new mother-in-law. And while Brian, Justin and Kylie weren't technically her children, she could understand a mother's distress.

"Angie and I are going to stop and see Chris in Red Rock while we're gone," Toby told her. "I'll talk to him."

"Thank you, son." She leaned in and kissed Toby right as another flash went off. "While you do that, I'll start working on your dad. And when these wedding pictures come back, I'll make a photo album to send to Chris. Maybe it'll remind him how much his family loves and misses him."

"Good idea."

"Can I have your attention?" the photographer asked. "I'd like to get one shot of everyone together. Let's gather around this tree. It'll make a good backdrop."

"Hey!" Justin chimed in. "Let's take it by the tree house instead. That way, some of us can climb up there and look down on you guys."

The photographed ignored the child, but Angie didn't. "Before the day is over, Justin, I'll have him take a family shot of the five of us near the tree house."

"How come we can't all be up in it?" Justin asked.

Angie caressed the top of his head. "Because I don't think I'd be able to climb very well in this dress."

"Five bucks says you can." Mr. Murdock, who stood beside her, nudged her with his elbow. "And another five says that I'll beat your time getting up there."

Angie laughed. "I'm not taking that bet, Mr. Murdock. This is going to be a wager-free wedding."

Before long, the reception launched into a full-scale party, with the food and drinks flowing freely.

When the DJ called the bride and groom to the dance floor, he said, "Since they didn't have a song picked out, I'll play a country classic."

"Seriously?" Toby called out. "Don't you have anything by Aretha Franklin? I'd take her over Patsy Cline any day of the week."

The whole dance floor fell into a hush, and Angie shook her head, realizing her husband had just said the one thing bound to agitate Texans quicker than a piñata at a five-year-old's birthday party.

"I'll see what I can do," the DJ said.

Moments later, as the music started, Toby and Angie stepped out onto the dance floor. Before long, other couples joined them—Stacey and Colton, Jude and Gabi, Liam and Julia.

Even Toby's cousin Amelia Fortune Chesterfield had found a dance partner in Quinn Drummond, who owned a ranch neighboring Toby's.

Quinn held Amelia close as Etta James crooned out through the speakers. The unlikely pairing of the proper British noble with a Horseback Hollow cowboy brought another smile to Angie's lips.

She nodded slightly and whispered, "Apparently, there's something about a wedding that makes for the strangest dance partners."

Toby drew her close. "And some of the nicest."

"You've got that right, cowboy." Then Angie wrapped her arms around her husband's neck and kissed him with all the love in her heart.

Two days later, in the honeymoon suite at one of San Antonio's swankiest hotels, Toby woke up with his wife in his arms, her back to his chest, her bottom nestled in his lap. Just hours ago, they'd made love again.

It seemed as though they couldn't get enough of each other, and he had a feeling that was how it was always going to be.

Today they planned to drive out to Red Rock, although he wasn't in any big hurry to let go of his lovely, naked wife.

"Are you awake?" he whispered against her hair.

"Um-hum." She arched and stretched. "I was just thinking."

Toby pressed a kiss on her bare shoulder. "What about?"

"About you and me and all the kids."

"All?" He chuckled. "I guess three would seem like a lot to an only child."

"Actually, I was thinking about the younger ones— the babies we're going to have."

"Babies? How many do you plan on having?"

"Well, none by myself. I was hoping you'd be involved."

He laughed. "I'm in this thing all the way, honey. So we can have as many kids as you'd like."

"I was thinking that six would be a good number."

"Six total?" he asked. "Or six more?"

Angie turned to face him, her smile radiant. "I'd like as many kids as we're blessed with."

"So the woman who once feared commitment is now daydreaming about having babies?"

"Yes. Little cowboys who are just like you—strong and handsome, loving and wise. And little girls who, like your mom, know that real wealth lies in love and family."

"Okay, but we'll need to have at least one little girl like you. One who's as inventive and creative and loving as she is beautiful." Toby pressed a kiss on Angie's brow. "Have I told you how much I love you?"

"Seven times throughout the night, but I'll never get tired of hearing you say it."

"Oh, yeah? Then you're really going to like it when I show you just how much."

Then he took her in his arms and did just that.

Toby had no idea what the future would bring, but right now, he was going to cherish every moment of the present.

* * * * *

*Don't miss the next chapter
in the new Special Edition continuity*

THE FORTUNES OF TEXAS: WELCOME TO HORSEBACK HOLLOW!

Christopher Fortune Jones has turned his back on his family in pursuit of fame and, well, fortune in Red Rock. But can his beautiful young assistant—with a troubled past of her own—teach him that money isn't everything?

*Look for
FALLING FOR FORTUNE,
by Nancy Robards Thompson.
On sale May 2014,
wherever Harlequin books are sold.*

COMING NEXT MONTH FROM

HARLEQUIN®

SPECIAL EDITION

Available April 15, 2014

#2329 THE PRINCE'S CINDERELLA BRIDE
The Bravo Royales • by Christine Rimmer
Lani Vasquez cherishes her role as nanny to the Montedoran royal children—
particularly since it offers proximity to her good friend, the handsome Prince Maximilian.
Max has grieved his lost wife for years, but this Prince Charming is ready for the next
chapter of his love story—and his Cinderella is right under his nose.

#2330 FALLING FOR FORTUNE
The Fortunes of Texas: Welcome to Horseback Hollow
by Nancy Robards Thompson
Christopher Fortune has gladly embraced the wealth and power of his newfound family
name. But not everyone's as impressed by the Fortune legacy. His new coworker,
Kinsley Aaron, worked for everything she ever got, and Chris's newly entitled attitude
rubs her the wrong way. Now Chris will have to earn Kinsley's love—and his Fortune
fairy-tale ending....

#2331 THE HUSBAND LIST
Rx for Love • by Cindy Kirk
Great job? Check. Hunky hubby? Not so much. Dr. Mitzi Sanchez has her life just where
she wants it—except for the husband she's always dreamed of. She creates a checklist
for her perfect man—but she insists pilot Keenan McGregor isn't it. With a bit of luck,
Keenan might blow Mitzi's expectations sky-high....

#2332 HEALED WITH A KISS
Bride Mountain • by Gina Wilkins
Both burned by love, wedding planner Alexis Mosley and innkeeper Logan Carmichael
aren't looking for anything serious when they plunge into a passionate affair. Little by
little, though, what starts as a no-strings-attached fling evolves into something much
deeper. Can they heal their emotional wounds to start afresh, or will the ghosts of
relationships past haunt them forever?

#2333 GROOMED FOR LOVE
Sweet Springs, Texas • by Helen R. Myers
Due to her declining sight, Rylie Quinn abandoned her dreams of becoming a
veterinarian and moved to Sweet Springs, Texas, as an animal groomer. She just wants
to get on with her life—something that irritating attorney Noah Prescott won't allow her
to do. He's determined to dig up Rylie's past, and, as he and Rylie butt heads, true love
might just rear its own.

#2334 THE BACHELOR DOCTOR'S BRIDE
The Doctors MacDowell • by Caro Carson
Bright, free-spirited and bubbly, Diana Connor gets under detached cardiologist
Quinn MacDowell's skin...and not in a way he'd care to admit. When the two are forced
to work together at a field clinic, Quinn begins to see just how caring Diana is and
how well she interacts with patients. This heart doctor might just need a bit of Diana's
medicine for himself....

_____

**YOU CAN FIND MORE INFORMATION ON UPCOMING HARLEQUIN® TITLES,
FREE EXCERPTS AND MORE AT WWW.HARLEQUIN.COM.**

HSECNM0414

REQUEST YOUR FREE BOOKS!

2 FREE NOVELS PLUS 2 FREE GIFTS!

♦ HARLEQUIN®

SPECIAL EDITION

Life, Love & Family

YES! Please send me 2 FREE Harlequin® Special Edition novels and my 2 FREE gifts (gifts are worth about $10). After receiving them, if I don't wish to receive any more books, I can return the shipping statement marked "cancel." If I don't cancel, I will receive 6 brand-new novels every month and be billed just $4.74 per book in the U.S. or $5.24 per book in Canada. That's a savings of at least 14% off the cover price! It's quite a bargain! Shipping and handling is just 50¢ per book in the U.S. and 75¢ per book in Canada.* I understand that accepting the 2 free books and gifts places me under no obligation to buy anything. I can always return a shipment and cancel at any time. Even if I never buy another book, the two free books and gifts are mine to keep forever.

235/335 HDN F45Y

Name   (PLEASE PRINT)

Address   Apt. #

City   State/Prov.   Zip/Postal Code

Signature (if under 18, a parent or guardian must sign)

Mail to the **Harlequin® Reader Service:**
IN U.S.A.: P.O. Box 1867, Buffalo, NY 14240-1867
IN CANADA: P.O. Box 609, Fort Erie, Ontario L2A 5X3

Want to try two free books from another line?
Call 1-800-873-8635 or visit www.ReaderService.com.

* Terms and prices subject to change without notice. Prices do not include applicable taxes. Sales tax applicable in N.Y. Canadian residents will be charged applicable taxes. Offer not valid in Quebec. This offer is limited to one order per household. Not valid for current subscribers to Harlequin Special Edition books. All orders subject to credit approval. Credit or debit balances in a customer's account(s) may be offset by any other outstanding balance owed by or to the customer. Please allow 4 to 6 weeks for delivery. Offer available while quantities last.

Your Privacy—The Harlequin® Reader Service is committed to protecting your privacy. Our Privacy Policy is available online at www.ReaderService.com or upon request from the Harlequin Reader Service.

We make a portion of our mailing list available to reputable third parties that offer products we believe may interest you. If you prefer that we not exchange your name with third parties, or if you wish to clarify or modify your communication preferences, please visit us at www.ReaderService.com/consumerschoice or write to us at Harlequin Reader Service Preference Service, P.O. Box 9062, Buffalo, NY 14269. Include your complete name and address.

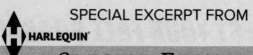
*Lani Vasquez is a nanny to the royal children of
Montedoro…and nothing more, or so she thinks.
But widower Prince Maximilian Bravo-Calabretti
hasn't forgotten their single passionate encounter.
Can the handsome prince and the alluring au pair turn
one night into forever? Or will their love turn Lani into a
pumpkin at the stroke of midnight?*

***

He was fresh out of new tactics and had no clue how to get
her to let down her guard. Plus he had a very strong feeling
that he'd pushed her as far as she would go for now. This was
looking to be an extended campaign. He didn't like that, but
if it was the only way to finally reach her, so be it. "I'll be seeing you in the library—where you will no longer scuttle away
every time I get near you."

A hint of the old humor flashed in her eyes. "I never scuttle."

"Scamper? Dart? Dash?"

"Stop it." Her mouth twitched. A good sign, he told himself.
"Promise me you won't run off the next time we meet."

The spark of humor winked out. "I just don't like this."

"You've already said that. I'm going to show you there's
nothing to be afraid of. Do we have an understanding?"

"Oh, Max…"

"Say yes."

And finally, she gave in and said the words he needed to
hear. "Yes. I'll, um, look forward to seeing you."

He didn't believe her. How could he believe her when she sounded so grim, when that mouth he wanted beneath his own was twisted with resignation? He didn't believe her, and he almost wished he could give her what she said she wanted, let her go, say goodbye. He almost wished he could *not* care.

But he'd had so many years of not caring. Years and years when he'd told himself that not caring was for the best.

And then the small, dark-haired woman in front of him changed everything.

***

Enjoy this sneak peek from Christine Rimmer's
THE PRINCE'S CINDERELLA BRIDE,
the latest installment in her Harlequin® Special Edition
miniseries **THE BRAVO ROYALES,** *on sale May 2014!*

HARLEQUIN®

SPECIAL EDITION

Life, Love and Family

Coming in May 2014

HEALED WITH A KISS
by reader-favorite author
Gina Wilkins

Both burned by love, wedding planner Alexis Mosley and innkeeper Logan Carmichael aren't looking for anything serious when they plunge into a passionate affair. Little by little, though, what starts as a no-strings-attached fling evolves into something much deeper. Can they heal their emotional wounds to start afresh, or will the ghosts of relationships past haunt them forever?

Don't miss the third edition of the
***Bride Mountain** trilogy!*

Available now from the
Bride Mountain trilogy by Gina Wilkins:

MATCHED BY MOONLIGHT
A PROPOSAL AT THE WEDDING